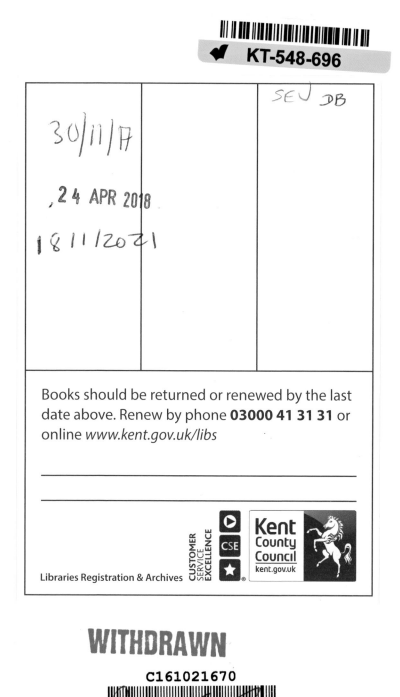

KT-548-696

SEU DB

30/11/A

24 APR 2018

18/11/2021

Books should be returned or renewed by the last
date above. Renew by phone **03000 41 31 31** or
online *www.kent.gov.uk/libs*

Libraries Registration & Archives

CUSTOMER
SERVICE
EXCELLENCE

CSE

Kent
County
Council
kent.gov.uk

THE SINNER'S
MARRIAGE
REDEMPTION

THE SINNER'S MARRIAGE REDEMPTION

BY

ANNIE WEST

First published in Great Britain 2015
by Mills & Boon, an imprint of Harlequin (UK) Limited,
Large Print edition 2015
Eton House, 18-24 Paradise Road,
Richmond, Surrey, TW9 1SR

© 2015 Annie West

ISBN: 978-0-263-25704-5

Harlequin (UK) Limited's policy is to use papers that
are natural, renewable and recyclable products and made
from wood grown in sustainable forests. The logging
and manufacturing processes conform to the legal
environmental regulations of the country of origin.

Printed and bound in Great Britain
by CPI Antony Rowe, Chippenham, Wiltshire

For Liz.
Amica carissima et doctissima,
and an admirable woman!

PROLOGUE

THE CAR'S ACCELERATION was loud in the still night, breaking the silence Flynn had so enjoyed after the bustle of London.

As he stretched his legs on a midnight walk across Michael Cavendish's country estate, the only sound should have been the swoop of an owl or the rustle of small creatures foraging. Flynn was too far from the big house for the sounds of the Cavendishes' annual winter bash to intrude.

The car roared closer, towards the tight bend in the long drive. Flynn quickened his pace, suddenly alert. It wasn't braking soon enough to make the turn.

By the time the sickening screech and thud of a collision shattered the night, Flynn was sprinting.

The drift of cloud across the moon parted as he scudded around the thicket on a surge of frantic adrenaline. There it was: an open convertible at an ungainly angle, nose deep in the dark foliage. Moonlight sparkled on shattered glass that crunched under his feet.

But Flynn's eyes were on the driver's seat. On the

figure struggling with the door. Moon-silvered hair spilled over pale, bare shoulders and arms flecked with what he suspected was blood. His heart hammered even as relief kicked in. At least she was conscious.

'Don't move.' He had to see how badly she was injured, and quickly.

'Who's there?' Instantly the woman shrank back from the door.

Her head snapped up and shock slammed into him. Ava? It couldn't be little Ava Cavendish. Not in that tight, low-cut white evening gown. Not with those lush breasts.

'Who is it?'

This time Flynn registered the sharp fear in her tone. Already she was trying to climb out the opposite side of the car, her long dress catching.

'Ava? It's okay. It's me, Flynn Marshall.' He reached the driver's door but couldn't wrench it open. The metal was buckled. Frustration surged.

'Flynn? Mrs Marshall's son?'

Her voice was slurred and anxiety stabbed him. Wasn't slurred speech a danger sign?

'Yes, Flynn.' He made his voice soothing as he tried to recall hazy first aid knowledge. 'You know me.'

A gusty sigh met the revelation. She mumbled something under her breath. He caught the word *safe*.

Flynn frowned. 'Of course you're safe with me.'

They'd grown up on the estate. Ava in the big house and he in a cramped workers' cottage with his parents.

'Here. This way.' He had to get her away from the car. He couldn't smell petrol but he'd take no chances.

Whatever her injuries, she could move her arms and legs. No spinal damage, hopefully. She'd already clambered up to kneel on the seat.

She twisted and a bottle dropped to the floor.

Since when had Ava been drinking champagne? She must be only—he did a quick mental calculation—seventeen. More to the point, the Ava he knew was far too responsible to drink and drive, even in a fit of teen rebellion.

'Sure you're Flynn?' She frowned owlishly, sitting back on her heels. 'You look different.'

Ava had never seen him in his city suit or anything as expensive as his cashmere coat. On his visits to his mother he reverted to casual clothes. Tonight, knowing his mother would be at the big house all night, working, he'd arrived late then set out for a stroll to clear his head after the drive. And to say farewell. This would be his last visit. Finally he'd convinced his mum to leave Frayne Hall.

'I'm definitely Flynn.' He reached out and scooped her up in his arms, lifting her carefully over the low door. But when he would have put her on her feet she clung tight, arms wrapped around his neck.

'You have to promise.'

Wide, bright eyes glittered up at him and something punched hard in his gut.

'Promise you won't take me back.'

'You need help. You're hurt.' Some of the dark streaks on her pale skin had smudged. Blood. *Hell!* He had to get her away from here, see how badly she was injured.

'*You* can help me. Just you.'

She pouted up at him, her glossy lips enticing even in the moonlight. To his horror he felt a ripple of masculine response.

'Please?'

She blinked and he saw tears fill her eyes.

He tightened his hold, valiantly ignoring the fact that little Ava had grown into a seductively luscious woman.

'Of course I'll help you.'

'And you promise you won't take me back? You won't tell them where I am?'

The intensity of her stare and the anguish in her voice raised the hairs on his nape.

She didn't sound drunk. She sounded scared.

He frowned, telling himself it was an illusion. She just didn't want to face the music. She'd crashed an expensive car and she'd been drinking. Yes, her father would be upset. Yet Flynn knew that Michael Cavendish, though an appalling employer, was a doting family man. Ava had nothing to fear.

'Promise me!' Desperation threaded her rising voice and she struggled in his arms.

Flynn looked towards the big house, a blaze of light in the distance. No one had come after her. They mightn't even know she'd left. He sighed.

'I promise. For now at least.' He'd take her to his mother's cottage, see how badly she was hurt, then decide whether to take her to a hospital and about ringing her father—the last man in the world he wanted to talk to.

'Thank you, Flynn.'

She smiled and laid her head against him. Her hair tickled his chin, the scent of roses and femininity curling around him.

'I always liked you. I knew I could trust you.'

Ava winced as she stepped into the cosy kitchen, awash with bright morning light. It wasn't that the light exacerbated her sore head so much as the fact it would reveal what she'd seen in the tiny bathroom mirror. Shadowed eyes. Bloodless lips now she'd scrubbed off her scarlet lipstick. Pale skin marked by scores of tiny cuts.

Far too much pale skin.

She'd tried to hitch her bodice up to cover herself a little more but it was no good. The dress was designed to reveal, not conceal.

The coward in her wished she could slip out without Flynn seeing her. He'd been marvellous, so supportive. But what must he think of her? Crashing her car, refusing to call her father or budge from his mother's cottage. She caught her breath. Would she have to face Mrs Marshall too this morning?

'Do you have a headache? I've got painkillers here.'

Ava swung around. Flynn stood, tall, dark and broodingly attractive, watching her with concern. He held out a glass and some medication. Her silly heart fluttered just at the sight of him.

Embarrassment surged. He'd anticipated she'd have a hangover. Could this scenario get any worse?

She wondered if he thought she did this all the time. Did he think she'd been wildly partying? She shivered.

Next thing she knew she was being gently pushed into a seat with something warm wrapped around her shoulders. It smelt fresh, like the forest after rain. Like Flynn. She breathed deep, his masculine scent going straight to her head.

'Thank you.'

Ava met his dark eyes, felt again that unfamiliar pulse of awareness before looking away. He overwhelmed her. From childhood she'd been drawn to Flynn, despite the seven years between them, to his devil-may-care adventurous streak and his kindness.

More recently, though, Ava had been tongue-tied by the assured, handsome man he'd become. Even his loose-limbed stride appealed. Did he know he made her heart beat faster? That she melted a little inside when he looked at her with those enigmatic dark eyes? That sometimes she dreamed—

'Water would be lovely, thank you.' She drew on years of self-discipline, projecting an assurance she didn't feel as she accepted the glass and the headache tablets, pretending that sitting in a ruined evening gown that left her half naked was in any way normal. 'Is your mother home?'

'No. She sleeps at the house when there's a big party and she has to be up early for the breakfasts.'

Ava nodded, trying not to think of what was happening up at Frayne Hall right now.

'Are you ready to talk about last night, Ava?'

Flynn's voice was low and soft, brushing across her skin like plush velvet. She loved the sound of her name on his lips. But she couldn't let him distract her.

'Thank you for helping me.' She put the glass down on the kitchen table. 'It's time I got back.'

'You're going to the Hall?' He frowned. 'Last night you were adamant wild horses wouldn't drag you there.'

'Last night I wasn't myself.'

'You don't want to talk about it? You were very upset.'

She froze. What, exactly, had she said? It would be too excruciating if Flynn discovered why she'd driven away from the Hall so recklessly last night.

'Ava? Don't you trust me?' He hunkered down beside her. He looked so appealing, so strong, that for a moment she wanted to confide everything.

Impulsively she reached out to touch his gleaming dark hair. At the last minute she stopped. He couldn't solve her problems. Only she could do that.

'Of course I trust you.' *He was the only man she did trust.* 'The way you helped me last night…I can't tell you what it meant to me.' She pasted on a smile. 'But I really need to go now.'

It was time to face the music. Alone.

CHAPTER ONE

Seven years later

FLYNN LEANED BACK in his seat, letting the shadows engulf him as he observed the tourists at the front of the boat. Eagerly they chattered, craning out over the Seine to get the perfect shot of Paris in the late-afternoon glow.

Only one of them was, like him, alone. She shoved her sunglasses up, pushing back wheat-gold hair to reveal a peaches and cream complexion in a heart-shaped face.

Even features, a straight nose and a mouth too wide for true beauty shouldn't arrest his attention. But Flynn tensed, each sinew and muscle tightening.

Animation had always lent a special appeal to Ava's face and now, when she smiled as Notre Dame passed by, her features were alive with pleasure.

Last time he'd seen her—the night she'd stayed in his mother's cottage after crashing her car—she'd still worn her youth in her features, despite her woman's body. He had felt guilty at the tug of attraction he'd experienced. Now, at twenty-four, high cheek-bones had emerged, giving her face a character and elegance only enhanced by that carefree smile…

Yet the intensity of his response surprised him. He hadn't expected that. It was a resonance deep within him—a quickening in his blood.

He frowned, trying to define the sensation. Attraction—yes. She was a good-looking woman. Not his usual style, though, in jeans and a bright floral shirt. He preferred women who projected glamour and restrained sophistication. But Ava could do that too. She'd been born and bred to it.

Flynn nodded. That was the explanation, of course. It was satisfaction he felt. Satisfaction that she really was the right woman. The perfect woman. He'd known within a moment of seeing her that this would work perfectly.

It was always good when a plan came together.

He watched her notice a couple embracing on the embankment, a wistful smile flickering across her mouth.

Curiously, for a moment doubt assailed him. Then he banished it and rose, making his way to the front of the boat.

When he reached her he paused and looked down. Eyes the blue of a perfect English summer afternoon

turned up to him, widening. Heat exploded in his
belly, swift and low, making him drag in air.

'Flynn?'

Her voice was husky with surprise. Delectable.

He smiled. He was a lucky man.

A week later Flynn again looked down into wistful summer-blue eyes and felt pleasure rise as Ava
reached for his hand. Slim fingers meshed with his
and he curled his possessively around them. *Yes!*

She looked so disappointed that he was leaving, but
equally determined not to show it. Silently he cursed
the work emergency that called him away. He was
so close. With a little more time—

'Of course you must go.' She nodded as if to make
up for her lack of enthusiasm. 'They need you in
London.'

'I know.' Though his business had grown vast he
was a hands-on CEO. He preferred to keep his finger on the pulse rather than delegate.

Now, though, Flynn regretted that no one else
could handle this latest problem. He didn't want to
leave Ava with nothing settled between them.

'Besides…' Ava tipped up her chin. 'I leave Paris
tomorrow for Prague.'

Did she know how much she revealed with that
brave, tight smile and those yearning eyes? In the

way she leaned in as if inviting him to scoop her close?

Satisfaction stirred. Perhaps his forced absence wasn't such a disaster after all. Perhaps it would work to his advantage.

CHAPTER TWO

AVA STUDIED THE GUIDEBOOK, telling herself it was good that she could explore Prague alone. She'd see more—not be distracted by dark eyes or Flynn's lurking smile.

Her week in Paris had been a blur of excitement and pleasure. Something out of a romantic dream.

But she'd known it couldn't last. Dreams never did.

When Flynn had been called away to London they'd parted with no plans to meet again. It had happened so fast she hadn't realised that till she'd been watching his broad shoulders cleave through the crowds on the Champs-Elysées, leaving admiring female stares in his wake.

He'd said nothing about the future. Had she just been convenient vacation company?

Ava's mouth tightened. It was ridiculous to experience this pang of longing. Yet she couldn't suppress a sigh. Paris, when he'd stayed on after his work meetings just to be with her, extending his few days into a week's stay, had been the most magical experience of her life.

Face it, Ava. It was the only magical experience you've ever had. Fairytales aren't for you.

She forced herself to scan the guidebook, reading about the defenestration of Prague, when irate locals had tipped three men out of this very castle window.

Defenestration. Such a pompous word. It reminded her of her father. Not that Michael Cavendish would have been caught committing assault. His speciality had been behind the scenes manipulation.

Ava snapped the book shut.

Life would have been better for a lot of people if someone had defenestrated Michael Cavendish years ago.

'Ava.'

She froze. Surely she was imagining that low voice, like dark chocolate and aged port.

She'd woken flushed and aroused this morning with that voice in her head. Drowsily she'd reached out, half believing she'd done what she hadn't dared to in Paris.

'Ava?'

Her head jerked up, then up again, and there he was—like the answer to a wish she hadn't dared formulate.

He stood, carelessly chic in bespoke casual clothes, looking at her with the tantalising hint of a smile. His saturnine good looks and an intriguing hint of unknowable undercurrents made Flynn Marshall the most compellingly attractive man she'd ever met.

Or maybe it was the gleam in sloe-dark eyes that spread warmth through her. That gleam hinted at shared secrets, a special bond.

'Flynn? I can't believe it!' Her smile widened. She hadn't a hope of concealing the tumultuous joy filling her chest so that for a moment she couldn't breathe.

It was as if all those years of learning to conceal her feelings and reveal only a poised, charming face to the world had never been.

With Flynn there was no need for the façade. She knew she was utterly safe with him.

If she experienced a frisson of danger it was delicious danger. A reminder that she was no longer a child but a woman and that he was potently, breathtakingly male.

'Why were you frowning? You looked grim.'

He brushed long fingers across her brow and something in her chest somersaulted. Ava told herself it couldn't be her heart, but she was past caring.

Flynn was here with her!

It couldn't be a coincidence. He'd had no plans to visit Prague. His business was in London.

'Ava?'

She blinked. 'I looked grim?' She'd been thinking of her father. No wonder she'd frowned. 'I was just reading the guidebook. Do you know this is where the defenestration of Prague took place? The second one. The first was down in the old town hall.'

Was she babbling? Probably. It was hard to concentrate with Flynn standing there, his eyes eating her up. Her flesh tightened, her nipples budding against her lace bra.

Surely he hadn't looked at her so hungrily in Paris. If he had she might have overcome a lifetime's scruples and invited him to—

'Perhaps it's a national pastime…tossing people out of windows.'

His low voice held the hint of a sexy chuckle. Ava felt it resonate through her. Or maybe that was a reaction to the deep green woodsy scent that was uniquely Flynn's. It did the strangest things to her.

'But the Czechs seem such friendly people,' she said.

'Who knows? Maybe they have hidden depths.'

Like Flynn.

They'd spent most of last week together in Paris and Ava had felt a connection she'd never experienced with any other man. Maybe because she'd known him when she was young—he'd been an older, intriguing figure, embodying the freedom she'd longed for. He'd been a true friend when she'd most needed one. She'd never forgotten his kindness that night of her father's party.

Yet she was aware there was a part of Flynn he kept to himself. But who didn't? Her own experiences had made Ava intensely private.

'You're looking serious again.'

Once more that fleeting touch stole her breath.

'I'm wondering what you're doing here. You had a crisis to deal with in London.'

Flynn shrugged and her gaze slid along straight, powerful shoulders. Heat trickled through her. She knew she had it bad when a pair of shoulders robbed her of breath.

'Ah. The emergency.'

But instead of explaining he stepped to one side, inviting her to follow. Immediately a family group took their place at the window, peering over the trees to the red roofs of old Prague.

Ava found herself standing with Flynn in a quiet corner beside another large window. She didn't glance at the view. Her attention was riveted on him.

With sharp cheekbones, deep-set eyes beneath slanted ebony brows and that strongly carved jaw, Flynn Marshall was enough to mesmerise any woman. His burnished skin hinted at his Romany heritage and the slightly askew set of his long nose, broken years ago, reinforced the aura of physicality in his athletic frame. Even the brutally short cut of his raven hair, which Ava knew would curl around his collar if left to grow, couldn't tame that hint of wildness.

A wildness that had transferred to her pulse. It racketed too fast.

'You were going to explain what you're doing here.' The words emerged sharply.

His mouth cocked up at one side in a half-smile that she felt in the sudden thump of her heart against her ribs. Ava gripped her book and took a step back—only to find herself against the window embrasure.

Flynn regarded her with laughing eyes, but for once Ava couldn't join in the joke. She felt clogged with anticipation, her chest constricting.

It wasn't Flynn's smile she wanted, but much more. How could she feel so much, want so much, after just a week?

The ache in her chest intensified and perversely Ava resented his effect on her. She hated feeling vulnerable. It was a sensation she'd worked hard to eradicate from her life.

It was a sensation she'd vowed never to feel again.

Ava lifted her chin, projecting something akin to the hauteur that had been her father's hallmark.

The laughter in Flynn's eyes died, leaving him sombre.

He raised his hand to touch her again but she stiffened. Opening up to Flynn as she had in Paris had been a completely new experience. Only now did she realise how dangerously far she'd let herself go.

'I came for you.' His voice brushed soft as a summer breeze across her sensitised skin.

'Me?' The word emerged from her constricted throat.

'You.'

He leaned closer but didn't touch her. He didn't need to. That glowing look melted her resistance and incinerated her doubts.

'I couldn't stay away, Ava.'

'But you had work to do—'

'I dealt with the crisis in a day and then rescheduled everything that wasn't critical.'

When he looked at her that way she was tempted to think he shared her feelings. Her breath hitched.

'One of the perks of being the boss?' She kept her tone light. 'Your secretary must love that.'

'I'm a good employer.'

She heard pride in his voice.

'And usually I'm easy to work with. I've never done this before.'

The air throbbed between them. Surely Flynn heard her heart pounding?

She swallowed, out of her depth. Carefree companionship teetered on the brink of something beyond her experience. Ava had played safe so long. She was torn between joy and fear at the prospect of stepping beyond her self-imposed boundaries.

'You've never played hooky before?' she teased, her voice uneven. It was easier to pretend she hadn't read his intense gaze. 'I find that hard to believe.'

He shook his head, that glimmer of a smile telling her he understood what she was doing.

No one apart from her brother Rupert read her so easily.

'I've done my share of rule-breaking.'

Flynn's defiance of the established order at Frayne Hall had been legend, and a favourite cause of complaint for her father. He'd accused his tenants' son of everything from poaching to disrespect and being 'too bloody clever for his boots'.

To Ava, seven years younger, his exploits had taken on mythic proportions—like those of Robin Hood and Zorro and every other defiant rule-breaker rolled into one. She'd applauded his audacity and mourned his absence when he'd left. She'd longed to follow in his footsteps and stand up to oppressive authority. Finally she had, but years of conformity had taken their toll.

'But not now you're a businessman?' It had been a shock to discover Flynn the maverick was now a respected businessman, doing something conventional in the City.

'I take calculated risks, but cancelling important appointments isn't my style.' The smile disappeared, his face suddenly serious. 'Until now. Until you.'

The heat in his eyes seared her from the top of her head to the tips of her toes.

'But I'll be back in London myself next week.' Her voice was croaky and she couldn't seem to get her breath.

Flynn shook his head. 'I couldn't wait that long.'

Ava's pulse sprinted at what she read in his eyes. He took her hand, lifting it to his lips, his gaze never wavering from hers.

It was the first time he'd kissed her.

In Paris she'd wondered if he might, hoped he would. She'd berated herself for not taking the initiative to kiss him.

In the background she heard voices, the echo of footsteps, but they barely registered. Her senses focused on those hard, warm fingers enfolding hers and the press of surprisingly soft lips sending ripples of pleasure up her arm.

Dark eyes glittered as he pressed a kiss to her palm, turning the ripple into a floodtide of delight.

Dazed, she shook her head. She wasn't a complete

innocent. She'd dated, shared kisses. But she'd never experienced anything so flagrantly erotic.

They were fully clothed, in a public place, yet with that simple caress Flynn had reduced her to quivering neediness. Except she didn't feel reduced. She felt buoyant, light as air, as if she'd swallowed sunshine.

'You came for me?' she whispered, afraid to believe it.

Despite her materially privileged upbringing, she'd never been made to feel special. To her father she'd been a commodity, not a person in her own right.

Flynn had cancelled a packed schedule to join her. No one had done anything like that in her life—put her first. It filled her to the brim with stirring emotions.

'I did come for you.'

Flynn's lips traced the words across her palm, making her tremble as arousal stirred.

'I told you I couldn't stay away.'

Her fingers touched his cheek, threaded through his springy short hair, revelling in the unique textures of him: the hardness of sculpted bone beneath taut flesh, the softness of his hair, his heat against her palm.

'I missed you.' With Flynn here her doubts seemed foolish. 'I was afraid I wouldn't see you again.'

He smiled, his expression so satisfied that for a moment it bordered on smug. But the impression was so fleeting she told herself she must have imagined it.

'I missed you too, Ava. Our week in Paris wasn't enough for me. I need more.'

Ava was still absorbing that when he bent, reaching for the floor. When he straightened he held the guidebook she hadn't noticed she'd dropped.

Heat flushed her cheeks as she took it. She'd never been clumsy—if she had it had been drummed out of her. She was twenty-four, competent, savvy, and never bowled over by men no matter how suave. *Especially* if they were suave. Life had taught her to be wary, even suspicious.

Yet with Flynn it was as if she were seventeen again—klutzy and breathlessly awakening to romance.

A seventeen she'd never been.

She tasted bitterness on her tongue. There'd been no room for romance or dreams then. Just harsh reality that had taught her good things came at a cost.

What was it about Flynn that cut through those hard-won lessons? The fact that he had nothing to gain from being with her? That he could have no ulterior motive? That his interest was in *her* and not, as so often in the past, in who she'd been?

Because Flynn was genuine.

Because she'd known him for ever.

Because he'd proved she could trust him.

How could she not? He'd helped her on the worst night of her life. Inspired her to change her life even if he hadn't realised it then.

'Thank you.' Ignoring the clinging shreds of caution that warned her to hold back, Ava smiled, letting her feelings show.

Flynn blinked and then, swift as thought, moved in to grasp her arm, his touch deliciously possessive.

'I was right to follow you to Prague.'

He paused, his expression making the blood hum in her veins.

'Wasn't I?'

For an instant she hesitated, unused to laying herself open. But these new feelings were too intense to ignore. Besides, wasn't being with Flynn what she'd longed for?

'Absolutely.' She curled her fingers around his arm, staking a claim of her own. It felt good.

'Seen enough here?'

Ava dragged her gaze from those velvety eyes, noticing for the first time the tourists casting them curious stares.

'Yes.' She dropped the guidebook into her tote bag and pressed close, revelling in the feel of him beside her. She felt ready to follow him anywhere.

Moments later they retraced her route through the

Vladislav Hall, so long and cavernous that in the old days knights had entertained the nobility here with indoor jousts.

Ava smiled as they headed for the exit, imagining Flynn astride a warhorse. Strangely, the image came easily. With his determination and athleticism he'd be a force to be reckoned with in combat. More, he'd look wildly romantic with his sculpted, dark features and glowing gaze as he accepted a lady's favour. *Her* favour.

She shook her head, dispelling the fantasy.

But nothing could dispel the heady sense that she'd left behind dull reality and entered a glorious new world to which Flynn held the key.

He drew her arm further through his, his smile melting her internal organs.

Did she have stars in her eyes? She didn't care.

For the first time in her life Ava was in love. Completely, head over heels in love.

Flynn was everything she'd never dared dream of: understanding, charismatic, funny, sexy, gently teasing, considerate yet strong. Caring.

She'd spent years distrusting men's motives. All her life, it seemed. But she knew Flynn. He'd never hurt her or play the heartless, manipulative games with which she'd grown up. He'd rescued her years before and never once tried to use her in any way.

Flynn was special. He always had been.

Why shouldn't she, for the first time ever, let her emotions rule? Fling away caution and live the dream? Even if it was scary, letting go.

Ava was tired of allowing the shadows of the past to restrict her life.

As they left the old palace and emerged into the sunlight of the citadel Ava felt she was stepping into her own private fairytale.

CHAPTER THREE

THEY WATCHED THE sun go down from a romantic outdoor restaurant perched high on a hill. Hand in hand they talked, laughed and sipped delicious local wine. If Ava spent more time drinking in Flynn's sculpted features rather than the view of orchards, ancient buildings and the glinting river, what did it matter?

Flynn's whole attention was focused on her. Ava had never felt so important, so...*treasured*.

The closeness they'd shared in Paris reached a new level. Even after such a short time they could finish each other's sentences. Ava revelled in the fact they understood each other so well.

Now, in the lobby of her small hotel, she didn't want the magic to end.

'Come up to my room?'

The words emerged breathlessly and Ava lifted her chin to counteract any hint of vulnerability. She was inexperienced, but that was from choice, not fear. Deliberately she banished all thought of why she'd remained celibate.

She wanted Flynn as she'd never wanted any man. Never thought she *could* want any man. She'd always had a weakness for him, since her teens.

Black eyebrows slashed down over eyes turned suddenly inscrutable. Surely Ava was mistaken in thinking, even for a fleeting second, that she'd seen calculation in Flynn's expression?

That was what a lifetime of distrust did to you.

Thrusting it aside, she took his hand. It was hard and warm as it gripped hers.

Fire arced through her when Flynn leant close.

'Lead the way.'

His words feathered her hair. Something twanged inside, like a string plucked, taut and vibrating. Ava's heart-rate raced faster.

Up and up they went. With each step she was ultra-aware of Flynn behind her, his body shadowing hers. The only sounds were the creak of stairs and her fractured breathing.

Finally they reached the small landing. His closeness made her skin prickle in anticipation. Waves of longing washed through her as she inhaled his warm, woodsy scent.

All afternoon and evening they'd been together, yet there'd been no pressure from him for more intimacy. That was a good thing. Here was a man interested in her thoughts and feelings, not just her body.

She was grateful Flynn hadn't rushed her. He was so physically imposing he could be almost daunting. Now she'd grown accustomed to his nearness and the feel of their fingers entwined, fitting so perfectly.

Was that how their bodies would fit?

Her breath quickened and grew shallow. Flynn might be giving her space, but she knew what she wanted even after such a short time. Nothing in her life had ever been so crystal-clear.

The old-fashioned key was heavy in her hands. She had to try twice before the lock clicked. She sighed with relief.

'You'll have to watch your head. I'm under the eaves so the roof slopes.'

Ava turned as she spoke to find him already in the room, the door closing behind him. In the dim light his tall frame filled the doorway and a frisson of sensation rippled through her. Doubt? Nerves? Excitement?

It made her hands clammy and her nipples peak against her bright T-shirt. Flynn's gaze dropped to her breasts and the air in her lungs whooshed out.

No, not doubt. Not with desire pooling in her belly. She *liked* it when he looked at her like that. It made her revel in her femininity.

In Paris she'd wondered about his feelings, but here

in Prague she'd seen the heat in his eyes, felt his possessive touch.

The key clattered onto the tiny bureau.

Flynn reached out and slid her tote off her shoulder, putting it beside the key. The brush of his knuckles against her top made her shiver expectantly.

She swallowed, suddenly gauche as their camaraderie disintegrated, incinerated by the flagrant heat of arousal. It scorched her to the core.

She'd never invited a man to her bed.

Before she could tie herself in knots with nerves, Ava stepped close. Flynn's hard body drew her and she put her palms on his solid chest, feeling heat sear through the fine weave of his shirt. *Yes!*

His heart beat reassuringly beneath her fingers. Ava just had time to register that his pulse was far steadier than hers when large hands clamped her hips, drawing her to him. Need rose in looping spirals through her middle as she watched him smile.

'You look like a cat about to swallow a bowl of cream,' she whispered.

'That's how I feel.'

Flynn's voice was a bass rumble she felt in the pit of her stomach. His thumbs circled her sides, just above the top of her jeans, making her hyperaware of every stitch of clothing and the fact that she wanted to be rid of them.

'Does that mean you'll purr for me?' She slid her hands up, linking them behind his neck. His skin was hotter than hers, more alive. Enticing.

Something flared in Flynn's eyes. Something that reminded her he was no domestic pet. Her heart hit an extra beat.

No doubt he was vastly experienced with women. She'd seen heads turn when he passed. He was a man supremely comfortable in his skin, with an incredibly sexy aura of physical assurance.

'Try me and see.'

He tugged till she was pressed against him, her breasts rising and falling against his torso. It was delicious.

Rising on her toes, Ava lifted her face, paused, reading the heavy invitation in his eyes, then skimmed her lips along his.

Soft, surprisingly cool. His mouth invited more. She paused, noticing for the first time the tiny tic of a pulse under his jaw that told her for all his cool Flynn was waiting, just as eager as she.

Ava tilted her head, planting her lips on his, moving tentatively as she learned the contours of his mouth.

He let her explore, standing passive. Almost passive—for his mouth responded, mimicking her gentle movements, inciting desire that drilled deep.

Ava slipped her tongue between his lips, finding warmth, heat, pleasure. She pressed closer, needing more, letting her body flatten against the intriguing contours of his frame. Bone and muscle and, yes... She twisted her hips. Arousal.

Instantly the hands at her sides clamped, drawing her tighter against him. His stance altered and somehow her body was curved into his, his head and shoulders were dominating, bowing her backwards, surrounding her.

The tempo of their kiss changed as Flynn gave up any pretence at passivity and took control, his mouth working hers, sucking, tasting, delving, drawing delight from every caress.

The world spun behind Ava's closed lids as sensations more potent than any she'd known racked her body.

It was like tasting a burst of fireworks. Luminous delight singed her, detonating at pulse-points through her primed body, urging her to enjoy, take more, give everything.

Lost in luscious ecstasy, Ava barely registered the softening of her body, the melting at her core. She only knew she needed more.

Hands sliding up through the thick, pelt-like softness of Flynn's cropped hair, she dragged his head closer, needily angling her face to his marauding mouth. Clumsy in her haste, her teeth mashed his lip and a sound of frustration broke from the back of her throat.

'Easy...' His voice was more vibration than sound.

Then all at once she was moving, pressed against the wall, caught between it and Flynn's hardness. Long fingers bracketed her jaw, holding her still as he plundered her mouth with an expertise that left her reeling.

Ava felt caged, at his mercy, and she loved it. Foggily she registered how wonderful it was to relax her defences and simply feel. She was intoxicated by him.

She hugged him tight. Muscles flexed beneath her fingertips, making her long for the feel of him naked.

Hunger surged.

She shivered, sensations rioting deep within. The scent of Flynn's skin, fresh like the outdoors, filled her nostrils and his taste, rich and addictive, made her greedy. Every neural pathway was clogged with the awareness of him—the texture of his skin, his heart beating strong and sure against her, the taut strength of his body pinioning her.

Then Flynn slipped his hand between them, moulding one aching breast, and her blood caught fire.

The sound of Ava's pleasure was part gasp, part sob, part roughened purr that trailed like cut velvet down his spine, drawing every nerve and sinew tight and hard.

And the taste of her! Sunshine and juicy ripe raspberries. She was like long-ago summers that never ended. And sex. Needy, greedy, heart-thumpingly satisfying sex.

Flynn's hold tightened on her soft breast and she pressed closer, her nipple a hard little nub against his palm. His heartbeat thundered in his head and his groin.

She responded so readily. She was flame in his hands, making him burn to the depths of his being.

He nudged her legs wider, insinuating his thigh where her heat beckoned, and she welcomed him, her kisses even more fervent.

Flynn groaned into her mouth. She was killing him.

Who'd have thought his delicate English beauty would be a raunchy tigress beneath the jeans and bright, spotted T-shirt? He'd spent a week biding his time, cautious not to overstep the bounds, fearing she might shy from anything too physical too soon. Yet here she was all but climbing his body, supple and eager and so very enticing.

So much for his careful planning!

Flynn rubbed his thumb over her peaked nipple and she shuddered, making his groin spasm. He slipped his other hand from her jaw and down, to cup her backside in those tight jeans, lifting her to cushion his erection. His heavy eyelids sagged as carnal hunger dragged at him.

He couldn't remember wanting any woman so fervently. It wasn't what he'd anticipated.

But he should have. He'd wanted her all those years ago, hadn't he?

'Flynn...'

It was a sigh and a promise. An invitation he couldn't resist.

He swung round towards the bed, holding her close—only to come up against the sloping ceiling.

'Are you okay?' Gentle fingers skimmed his head.

'Fine.'

Already he was scanning the twin beds against the far wall. *Twin beds!* Ava must have booked this room when she'd still expected to share with the girlfriend who'd taken ill and couldn't travel.

Ava wriggled, her thighs clamping his, and his brain refocused instantly.

They didn't need a bed. The floor would do—or, yes, *here*.

Flynn turned, imprisoning her once again against the wall. He slipped his hand from her buttocks round her hip, then down between her legs. Only taut denim and whatever flimsy underwear she wore separated him from the place he wanted to bury himself. She tilted her pelvis into his touch and fire roared through him.

The first time would be fast and hard, but then he'd take his time, learning every exquisite inch of her.

Flynn took her mouth with his, demanding, urging, and Ava responded without hesitation.

Her eagerness was tempered with a slight awkwardness he found faintly endearing. How long since he'd had a woman so obviously inexperienced? Not since his first fumbling assignation in his teens. After a diet of skilful sophisticates Ava was an entrancing breath of fresh air.

Hadn't he known from the first she was the perfect woman for him?

He'd stroked his hand to the top of her zip when something made him stop. Some sound just discernible through the rush of blood in his ears. Voices. A door slamming. He frowned, lifting his head.

'It's okay—just someone in the next room,' Ava whispered against his throat.

Flynn squeezed his eyes shut as the voices continued, followed by the sound of music. The walls must be made of cardboard.

Behind him a door banged, loud enough that for a moment he thought someone had entered the room. But it must be someone across the landing.

Hell!

'Flynn?'

Ava's soft hand stroked his jaw. Even that innocent touch was almost enough to jettison his doubts and obliterate his uncharacteristic hesitation.

Until he opened his eyes and found himself staring into wide cerulean eyes. They were glazed with the same heat he felt, but there was doubt too, a question he'd never seen in the eyes of the women he took to bed.

But Ava wasn't like them. She was an innocent.

The word hit his chest like the blow of a sledgehammer, robbing him of breath.

Flynn hadn't missed the almost imperceptible distance she'd kept between them in Paris, even when her eyes shone with laughter and her body language told him she wasn't immune to him. The stunned delight on her face when he'd kissed her hand today, her almost defiant expression when she'd invited him up here and her passionate kisses, with that slight edge of eager clumsiness, all confirmed it.

Ava wanted him but she was sexually inexperienced. He'd lay odds she was a virgin.

Twenty-four and a virgin. How was it possible?

She leaned in and nuzzled his throat, planting small open-mouthed kisses that turned his body to steel and threatened the last vestige of his control. She rubbed his back in needy arcs and his jeans shrank as her palms came to rest on his buttocks.

His head spun as her grip tightened.

Once more his gaze shifted to the cramped beds. Laughter sounded from the next room and with a sinking feeling Flynn felt his dormant conscience stir.

He didn't care if the neighbours heard them having raunchy, scream out loud sex against the wall. He didn't give a damn if he had Ava on a bed or the floor or up against this wall. So long as he had her.

But this wasn't just about him.

This would be Ava's first time.

He couldn't dislodge the thought.

Instinct urged him to forget pointless scruples and take what he wanted. What they both wanted. The way she rubbed herself against him made it clear she was as desperate as he. It would be easy to tip her over the edge, give her the satisfaction they both craved, even in such unprepossessing surroundings.

His lips twisted in self-mockery. Was it selfishness or experience that told him he could please her so well that embarrassment and discomfort wouldn't matter, even when the afterglow faded?

'Flynn.'

Those luscious lips pressed against his and he felt

his resolve drain. He could barely believe it when he grasped her by the elbows and stepped back. His body screamed denial at the loss of her lush body, those soft lips and eager hands.

Flynn swallowed. His throat worked over arid gravel.

'What is it? What's wrong?'

Ava wore the heavy-lidded look of arousal, her lips dark red from their kisses.

Pain cramped his groin at what he was giving up.

'Nothing's wrong.' Yet his voice wasn't his own. It was the growl of a wounded, hungry bear denied food.

She swayed closer and his hold tightened. He stepped away, watching the haziness fade from her eyes.

'This isn't a good idea.'

If there'd been any lingering doubt about Ava's inexperience the rosy flush to her throat and cheeks would have eradicated it.

Contrarily, Flynn found himself for the first time in his life turned on by the idea of a blushing virgin. Excitement that bordered on avarice hammered in his veins. He revelled in the knowledge that he'd be Ava's first.

Just not now. She deserved better.

'You mean—?'

'Not here. Not now—like this.' His gesture took in the wafer-thin walls and cramped quarters.

It struck him in that instant how much her life had changed since they'd first known each other. Then she'd never stayed anywhere except in five-star luxury.

Yet she hadn't once complained about her altered circumstances. Instead she'd been upbeat about the chance to visit Prague on her two weeks' vacation.

Ava's chin hiked up. 'If I don't mind...'

'But I do.' He couldn't keep his hands off her. Even pouting, she was delectable. His fingers trailed her throat, up to that argumentative chin. He had to repress a smile at her sensuous shiver. She was patently his for the taking.

He couldn't believe he was doing the noble thing. It didn't gel with his plans or his inclinations.

Yet he stepped away before he was tempted to haul her back against him. The half-dazed, half-angry expression she wore didn't help. He wanted to wipe it away and replace it with that yearning look that made him feel larger than life.

His hands clenched, then spread wide.

'I'd better go.' Already he was moving away, his steps ludicrously stiff because of his erection.

The shocked, mutinous look on her face told him he should say more but for once words deserted him.

It was all he could do to walk away. Yet something inside, something he hadn't listened to in a long time, told him he was doing the right thing.

'I'll see you tomorrow, Ava.'

CHAPTER FOUR

'*SEE YOU TOMORROW.*'

Ava winced. Flynn had left her so casually.

Indignation welled, as it had all night. She avoided the mirror, knowing what she'd see. Anger, but disappointment too, and a flush that felt disturbingly like arousal. All night she'd been troubled by dreams that left her achy and longing.

Her lips pursed. What had she done wrong? Surely she hadn't misinterpreted his eagerness.

She shook her head. She was doing it again: rehashing last night's mortifying scene where he'd all but had to prise her hands off him.

As for his tight-lipped look as he'd said, '*Not here, not now...*' It was naïve to think he'd been put off by their surroundings. Flynn might wear hand-made shoes and exquisitely tailored clothes, but he came from a working class family. She'd seen their modest cottage on the estate. There'd been nothing pretentious about the Marshalls.

Whatever made him leave last night it wasn't her room. That only left *her*.

Pride told her it was ridiculous to think she was so unattractive she'd scared him off. He hadn't found her unattractive when he'd kissed her.

Unless he hadn't really wanted to.

She'd invited him to her room.

She'd initiated the kiss.

Could she have got it wrong?

A knock at the door ended her circling thoughts.

Flynn? Her pulse thudded and she knew a cowardly desire to pretend she hadn't heard. Angry with herself, she put her shoulders back and marched to the door.

The man standing there was a foot shorter than Flynn and twice as wide. He held a boxed arrangement of exquisite peonies and camellias.

'Miss Cavendish?'

At her dazed nod he smiled and thrust the arrangement into her arms. Then with a half-bow he turned and headed downstairs before she had time to recover.

Cradling the flowers, Ava backed into her room. They were so perfect they didn't look real. But as she stroked a finger across one petal she was rewarded with a rich silken texture no man-made process could duplicate.

With unsteady hands she put them on the table. At

once her small room morphed from economy class to luxurious and exotically enticing.

She plopped onto the bed.

In twenty-four years she'd never been given flowers. How pathetic was that? Men she'd dated had wanted to buy her drinks or meals, but never anything as romantic as flowers. These weren't just romantic, they were flagrantly, unashamedly so.

An image surfaced of blood-red long-stemmed roses in an expensive florist's box. Ava shuddered and thrust the memory away. Those hadn't been a gift. They'd been a statement of possession.

She wrapped her arms around herself to dispel an inner chill and stared at the blooms—lush, sensual and gorgeous. She plucked the card from them.

They reminded me of you.

No signature, but they had to be from Flynn.

Ava blinked. They reminded him of *her*? She looked at the voluptuous splendour of the peonies, full-bloomed and extravagant, yet with their soft pink tint so delicate and feminine. And the camellias— pure white and elegant.

She frowned. Lush and voluptuous or neat and virginal?

How *did* Flynn view her?

Her figure was feminine, but hardly voluptuous. As

for virginal—heat rose in her cheeks. Flynn couldn't know that.

The trouble was she didn't know where she stood with him.

She'd lost her habit of keeping men at a distance the minute Flynn had smiled at her in Paris. With his charm and their shared history he'd broached every defence she'd built against glib, grasping men. The speed of their romance *had* stirred anxiety. But until last night she'd overridden it, too delighted and excited to care.

She'd thought she knew him. Till he'd left her so abruptly.

What was she going to do about him?

More, what could she do about her feelings for him? They tied her in knots and turned her well-ordered life and everything she knew about herself on their head.

Ava slipped on her sunglasses as she left the hotel and stepped onto the quiet cobblestoned street. She'd taken three paces when a tall shadow peeled away from the pastel-washed building opposite.

Flynn. Her heart beat a tattoo up high near her throat, robbing her of air.

'Forgive me?'

Eyes of black velvet snared her.

'What for? Sending flowers?'

'For walking out on you.'

Despite the glow in his eyes there were harsh lines bracketing his mouth, as if from tension or regret. Or maybe she was reading things that weren't there.

Ava shrugged airily and donned the polite society mask she'd perfected in her teens.

'Of course you're angry.'

Ava's brows rose. No one except Rupert had ever penetrated what she thought of as her armoured look—but then Rupe had grown up in the same family, suffering like her. He knew poise and surface charm didn't tell the whole story.

'I'm sorry.' Flynn's voice was a soft, deep rumble.

Instantly her nipples beaded and heat melted between her thighs, as if she were ready to continue where they'd left off last night. Her lips firmed at her body's betrayal. How could she? No man had ever made her weak like this.

'If it's any consolation it was the hardest thing I've ever done, walking away last night.'

His eyes mesmerised, willing her to believe him.

'Then why did you?'

His mouth kicked up at the corner in a rueful half-smile that infuriatingly made her body hum.

'You deserved better.'

'Better than you?' In her besotted state Ava couldn't

imagine anyone better than Flynn. That only fuelled her anger.

Slowly he shook his head, his gaze so intense she felt it like a wave of warmth, engulfing her from her head to her soles.

'Never that. The thought of you with another man…' Heat flickered in his eyes and Ava's breath hitched as his expression turned possessive. 'No. I couldn't stand it.'

Some primitive part of her psyche revelled in his discomfort, his possessiveness, even as she reminded herself that no man had the right to control her.

'I meant you deserved better than a cramped bed with the neighbours listening to every gasp and cry, hearing you in ecstasy and imagining exactly what we were doing with each creak of the mattress springs.'

The heat low in Ava's body shot, fizzing and supercharged, through every artery and capillary. It branded her body in fiery heat as her imagination provided pictures to go with Flynn's description. He'd be naked, strong and lithe, his hands sure, his body unflagging, as he took her to heights she'd never experienced.

Her palms tingled, her fingers tightening as if needing to reach out and touch.

It took far too long to dispel the erotic images he'd stirred.

'Surely I'm the best judge of that.' Her voice sounded throaty and full, disturbingly needy. 'You shouldn't have just walked out.' Too late for pride, but her feelings for Flynn made pride seem insignificant. It was honesty she craved.

'I know.'

He brushed her jaw in the lightest of caresses and she swallowed hard. Only indignation kept her from swaying into his touch.

'It was appalling behaviour. My only excuse...' his voice dropped to a deliciously deep whisper '...is that if I hadn't walked out there'd have been no time for scruples. I'd have had you fast and hard and very, very loud up against the wall, pounding into you with all the finesse of a horny teenager. I wouldn't have been satisfied until I had your legs around my waist and you were screaming my name in ecstasy.'

Ava felt her eyes widen, her heart stuttering at the graphic image. She sucked in a searing breath, watching him watch her absorb his words.

'What would have been wrong with that?' She didn't bother to hide her pique.

His lips curved in that smile she knew so well. His huff of laughter dispelled the shadows in his eyes.

He stepped in till she was encompassed by him, barricaded from any passing pedestrians.

'Nothing.'

Flynn's smile held that hint of wildness she'd always associated with him. Now, turned on her, it produced a frisson of doubt, the unease of a deer spying a hunter.

'It would have been glorious.'

His gaze dipped to her breasts, peaking against her colourful cotton shirt. Ava wanted to wrap her arms around her breasts, hide their burgeoning response. She wanted even more to revel in his hot hunger.

Suddenly his eyes meshed with hers. 'Except you would have regretted it later. When it came time to disentangle our bodies and straighten our clothes you would have been uncomfortable—especially knowing everyone on the floor had heard you come apart in my arms.'

He was right. She would have been uncomfortable. But she couldn't imagine for an instant regretting making love with Flynn. Not when she regretted so much *not* making love with him.

Flynn's hand settled at her waist, making her soften despite herself.

'I want our first time to be perfect. I want to pamper you and make you feel special. Not like some cheap one-night stand after a hot and heavy date.'

Hot and heavy would do it for her right now, but there was magic in the picture he painted. He wanted to make her feel *special*. No one had ever wanted that.

Ava was entranced by the idea as much as by the determination stamped on his dark features.

He wanted her. Her doubts had been ridiculous. She saw desire branded on his face. Excitement stirred like a whispering summer breeze, riffling through her.

'Besides…' He leaned in, his breath caressing her ear, sending shivers of delight through her primed body. 'I want your first time to be memorable in the very best way.'

It took a moment to absorb his words. Ava jerked her head back, shock stiffening her body. He *couldn't* know. No one but she knew that she'd never had sex. It wasn't branded on her forehead!

'What do you mean, my first time?' she hissed. Mortification hovered at the thought that she'd given away her inexperience—she who'd learned to project sophistication so early.

Flynn regarded her steadily. 'Virginity is nothing to be ashamed of.'

'I'm not ashamed,' she bit out, too late realising she'd confirmed his suspicions.

He nodded. 'Good.' He trailed his knuckles down

her hot cheek, his stare once more proprietorial. That look did strange things to her internal organs. It felt as if they were melting. 'I find the idea utterly entrancing.'

His palm settled at the base of her throat, his fingers caressing skin turned suddenly hyper-sensitive.

'You have a thing about virgins?' The words shot out, terse and abrasive. Did his look smack of the sick gloating she'd seen years ago, that last fateful night at Frayne Hall? Then she'd been slavered over like some tasty morsel. A thing, not a person.

'Ava? What is it?' Flynn's voice was sharp.

The air clogged in her throat, depriving her of breath.

'Talk to me.' It was an order, and it worked, jerking her out of sordid memory and into the present—the quiet street, the big, charismatic man with concern written on his wrinkled brow.

'It's nothing.'

It was a lie, but the alternative—spilling that ancient secret—was untenable. It made her feel tainted.

Ava dragged in air to fill her lungs. 'I don't like the idea it's my virginity you're interested in, not me.'

'That's what's bothering you?'

His face cleared. He captured her hand, lifting it. His tongue laved the centre of her palm, right up to her wrist, and she shivered as her body caught alight.

'Believe me, virgins per se don't tempt me. It's you I want, Ava. And not just in bed.'

Sincerity blazed in his face, and she felt her doubts crumble.

'What *do* you want, Flynn?'

Last night she'd felt on the brink of something—not just sex, but understanding this man who'd transformed her life from ordinary to heady and exciting. If she'd been prone to fantasy she'd have likened him to Prince Charming, sweeping all before him. But Prince Charming with an earthy edge and, despite his suave cloak of wealth, a hint of the maverick about him still. And, just occasionally, a hint of ruthlessness that gave her pause.

Flynn straightened, glancing over his shoulder, reminding her they were crammed against a wall in a nearly deserted street.

'Come with me.' He clasped her hand in his and took a half-step back. 'I have something organised that I think you'll like. We can discuss this then.'

Ava stood her ground. She needed answers. With Flynn she teetered between absolute certainty that they were two halves of a whole, made for each other, and the rare but unnerving idea that she'd missed something vital. That their relationship wasn't the wildly romantic affair it seemed.

She had to know.

'Tell me now. I need to understand.'

Night-dark eyes scanned her face, coming to rest on her mouth. Was her bottom lip sticking out? Her father had accused her of ugly pouting if she ever showed a hint of rebellion.

But Flynn didn't look at her as if she were ugly. The heat in his stare sent tingles through her. The air between them fizzed with energy.

'Please, Flynn.'

Did he hear her yearning?

He smiled ruefully, shaking his head. 'I had it all planned. It wasn't going to be like this.'

'*What* wasn't going to be like this?'

There it was again—that look in his eyes that told her Flynn wasn't like the city suits her father had mixed with. Despite his designer gold watch, expensive clothes and high-powered business meetings there was something elemental about Flynn.

To her amazement, he dropped to his knees on the cobblestones. To one knee, to be precise. His wry half-smile drove a cleft down his cheek, almost distracting her from the remarkable sight of him kneeling before her.

Once more he raised her hand to his mouth and his lips pressed her flesh. The hint of humour disappeared.

'Will you marry me, Ava?'

Her stomach swooped and did an unnerving loop the loop. Her hand began to shake in his.

'I want you in my bed, sweetheart. But I want much more. I want you to be my wife.'

'I…' She goggled. Never in her wildest dreams had she expected a proposal. Her heart soared. Flynn wanted to spend his life with her. He cared more than she'd ever guessed possible.

But *marriage*!

'We've only known each other a week.'

His brows rose. 'We've known each other for years.'

But how well? Seven years older than her, he'd usually been busy helping his father on the estate grounds, or running errands for his mother in the Hall kitchen. After he'd left for London she'd only seen him on brief visits home.

Yet despite that, she'd known his character. His integrity.

Then there'd been the night of the car crash. The night that had changed everything. Flynn had no idea how much his help had meant to her. Not merely because of the accident but because he'd given her time and respite to see that she'd had to go back and face her demons.

He'd cared for her as no one in that house had.

His support had strengthened her.

She'd been half in love with him even then.

Was it any wonder she'd fallen for him now? He embodied all she craved in a man: honour, respect, trust. Passion.

'But…marriage!'

Still he knelt. He showed no self-consciousness.

'You don't like the idea?'

'I've never thought of it.' She'd never daydreamed of weddings—probably because she'd seen the reality of her parents' marriage and knew it for a prison sentence, not a happy-ever-after. Even now, when she was in love with Flynn, the idea of marriage made her hesitate.

'Think about it,' he murmured. 'You and me together.'

His eyes were smoky with passion and Ava gulped. Outrageous as the sudden proposal was, it was shockingly tempting. To be with Flynn always…

'I need time,' she blurted, then waited for his gaze to turn needle-sharp. When her father hadn't immediately got his own way he'd had a look that could slice you off at the knees.

Flynn merely nodded and rose. 'Of course.'

He looped her arm through his. His touch reassured, but the way he held her to his side smacked of possessiveness.

Instead of it rankling, Ava revelled in it. Flynn *loved* her! Shock mingled with delight.

'Come on. There's somewhere I want to take you. We can talk there.'

'There' turned out to be a luxurious terrace restaurant on the river. They had a perfect view of the Charles Bridge with its statues, the quaint Bridge Tower rising at one end and the old town. Swans and small craft glided across the glinting river.

Magically, although it was lunchtime, they had the place to themselves. Or perhaps not so magically. Ava saw the head waiter turning people away from the door.

'Did you book out the whole restaurant?' She gasped, half laughing at the absurdity of the idea.

Flynn took her hand across the starched white linen tablecloth, his touch warm, his eyes mesmerising. 'I wanted to be alone with you.'

'But...' She knew he was successful. The little he'd told her about his business and the clothes he wore told her that. But to book an entire restaurant—moreover, one with such an air of exclusive luxury...? 'Really?'

'Really.' He must have read her shock. 'Don't worry, I can afford it. But I'd much rather talk about us.'

Ava's breath expelled in a fluttering sigh. *Us*. It sounded so good.

Flynn raised his crystal wine glass. 'To our future together.'

Automatically she lifted her glass. 'To the future.'

He smiled. 'You're still not sure.'

She took her time sipping the pale gold wine, tasting fruit, flinty soil and sunshine. Bubbles burst on her tongue and went straight to her head. Or perhaps that was the Flynn effect. When she was with him nothing seemed mundane or ordinary.

'I'm still stunned. We don't even know if we're physically compatible.'

His expression altered, focused, igniting wildfire in her veins. 'I think last night proves we've got no problems there. We're combustible together.'

He stroked her wrist and she shivered. Her need for him was a gnawing ache.

'But marriage is about more than physical attraction.'

Why was she arguing? She'd fallen for Flynn so completely she should be floating in seventh heaven. But a lifetime's caution couldn't be shucked aside in an instant.

'You don't think we're compatible? You haven't enjoyed our time together?'

'Of course I have. It's been…wonderful. I've never felt like this. But it's only been a week.'

'How long do you need to be sure? A month? A year?' Flynn put down his wine and leaned forward, shifting a platter of exquisitely presented appetisers. 'I knew the moment I saw you in Paris.'

Ava's breath caught. Love at first sight? It sounded impossibly romantic.

Yet it was there in his face: absolute certainty. Her heart flipped over.

'You care for me that much?'

'You're the one woman in the world for me, Ava. I've never wanted anyone else as my wife. You're perfect in every way. Perfect for me.'

She heard the harsh edge of emotion in his voice.

'You make me complete.'

'Flynn…' Her fingers meshed with his as he took her glass and put it on the table. Then he lifted her onto his lap with such negligent strength she would have been impressed if she hadn't already been dazzled by his words and the gleam in his eyes.

'Is it because *you* don't care enough for *me*?'

His lips brushed her ear, making her shiver.

'I care, Flynn. You know that.'

Despite a lifetime's training in bottling up emotions, Ava had let her feelings show time and again.

With Flynn, for the first time, that hadn't seemed to matter. What they had was real and precious. Honest.

His smile was so smug she laughed, sudden elation swamping doubt.

'Then say yes and I'll give you the biggest, best wedding London can provide. The church, umpteen bridesmaids and a lavish reception. I can see you in white, with a long train and—'

'No!' She tensed, a flake of arctic frost drifting down her spine, chilling her.

'Ava? What is it?'

She shook her head, trying to clear the shreds of dismay. 'No big wedding. No white dress.'

'But you'd look lovely.'

Flynn's voice was warm as syrup but it failed to dispel the cold creeping into her bones.

'No.' She met his questioning stare. 'Not white.'

Memory flashed an image of the long white evening gown she'd worn for that last winter ball at Frayne Hall. When she'd opened the couturier's box she'd thought it pretty, almost virginal. But it had clung like a glove, displaying her to hungry eyes. As it had been designed to do, she'd discovered later.

She shuddered.

'Not white, then.'

Flynn looked puzzled, but Ava wasn't about to enlighten him. She'd rather shove the past back where it belonged—in the past—and get on with her life.

'If I marry…' She paused, making sure he heard her conditions. 'I don't want lots of bridesmaids or fuss. No big wedding.'

'Surely you'll want all your friends and family to celebrate with you?'

Ava shook her head. She had a couple of good friends. She'd learned years ago to discern between those few genuinely interested in her and those attracted by her family's status and money. When the money bled away so did they. As for family, there was only Rupert and he was in America. Her parents were dead.

'No. If I marry I'd rather elope. Just a quiet, simple wedding.'

'There was I, thinking you'd revel in lace and roses. I thought you a romantic.' His tone was light but his expression was serious, as if he'd read her tension.

She shrugged. 'I love lace and roses. I just don't like a public fuss over something private.'

'So you'll marry me?' He tilted up her face.

Black velvet eyes caressed her and Ava's body softened. A sigh funnelled up from her lungs and she wanted to lean into him, surrender to passion, trust him totally.

But marriage…

'I need time to think about it.'

Even as she said it a voice cried inside that she was a fool. She loved Flynn. She wanted him. She had to learn to trust some time, didn't she?

His smile was endearing, his stroking fingers along her cheek infinitely tender.

'Then it's a good thing I'm an expert at persuasion.'

CHAPTER FIVE

FIVE DAYS LATER they were married in Prague.

Ava gripped Flynn's hand tight, following the prompts in a civil ceremony that should have been unemotional with its speed and lack of family or friends. Instead its simplicity concentrated the power of the vows they made.

Ava's heart rose as Flynn tenderly brushed his lips against hers. The kiss was butterfly-soft but there was no mistaking the fierce restraint he imposed to keep it so. His dark eyes glittered as he clasped her waist tight, his large hands splayed, his heat seeping into her. His shoulders were rigid as steel beneath his suave tailoring.

Soon, that look promised.

Heat arced between them and she trembled, heart full and her body at such a pitch of desire she wondered if it were possible to die of sexual frustration.

For five days Flynn had refused to do more than cuddle, or kiss her in some public place where there was no chance of giving in to the hunger spiralling between them.

Because he wanted their wedding night to be special, he'd declared.

If she hadn't known better Ava might have suspected he'd used the sensual tension between them as a lever to persuade her to marry him quickly.

Her hands cupped his neck and she looked into eyes that glowed with triumph. She felt the same elation. She'd made the right decision. Despite the whirlwind speed of their romance, she knew Flynn was the only man in the world for her.

'Come on, Mrs Marshall,' he murmured with that crooked smile that made her heartbeat hitch. 'It's time for photos.'

'Do we have to?'

Flynn laughed, the sound so infectious that Ava found herself smiling. He stroked his fingers down her cheek and her laughter faded. Just his touch turned her knees to jelly.

'I want pictures to show the grandkids.' His voice dropped, became husky. 'You look so perfect I want a memento.'

'No one's ever called me perfect.' Such extravagant praise was unsettling. 'I'll settle for pretty.'

In her tea length gown of palest gold silk covered with matching lace, she *felt* pretty. Not sophisticated, as her father had always insisted upon, but pretty and carefree. The wide circular skirt and cinched waist made her outfit fun in a retro style. The long, fitted lace sleeves with rows of miniscule buttons were deliciously feminine.

How Flynn had conjured it up, and the matching satin and lace shoes, in her exact size in mere days, she didn't know. But, instead of facing an ordeal by bridal gown, Ava had taken one look inside the garment bag and found herself grinning.

He'd listened when she'd said no white. He'd remembered her weakness for lace and roses. Fragrant gold and cream roses made up the posy she carried and were also tucked in her loosely upswept hair.

'Not just pretty,' Flynn said as he tucked her arm in his, leading the way through the town hall. 'Beautiful. Stunning. Perfect.'

Again that word. But Ava was too lost in wonder to cavil. For they'd entered a small high-vaulted room that took her breath away. Ceiling and walls were covered with glittering mosaics. Scenes adorned the walls and overhead were intricate heraldic designs. It was a jewel of a room.

'Now, if the bride could sit near the window?' A photographer gestured to a bench seat positioned against one decorated wall where sunlight slanted.

Ava paused. It wasn't a photo of herself she wanted, but a memento of the pair of them.

'Sit with me?'

Flynn nodded. 'Soon. Let her get a photo of you first.'

One photo turned into scores, but Ava didn't argue. Not when Flynn stood there, hands in pockets, surveying her as if he couldn't keep his eyes off her. It was his expression, rather than the lace and flowers and the unfamiliar weight of her wedding band, that made her feel like a blushing bride. To be the utter focus of his attention, to *feel* his regard with every breath—it was something she'd never dared dream of.

'Wonderful!' The photographer moved closer, her camera clicking. 'Just wonderful.'

Finally they emerged, arm in arm, into the cobblestoned square just as the astronomical clock on the tower chimed the hour. Tourists swung their cameras around from the clock to them as they stepped across gold and cream rose petals to an open horse-drawn carriage. Matched greys sported cream and gold feathers above their halters and garlands of pastel roses decked the carriage.

'You've pulled out all the stops, Mr Marshall.' Ava grinned up at Flynn. He'd turned their quiet wedding into pure romance, but he'd avoided the shallow society fuss she detested.

She covered his hand with hers. 'Thank you. It's all so gorgeous.'

'I'm glad you approve, Mrs Marshall.'

It didn't matter that he had the money to make all this happen. What mattered was that he'd listened to her and made the day special. Was it any wonder she'd fallen hard for this man who treasured her so?

Ava paused on the step up to the carriage. She leaned in, her lips grazing his ear. 'I love you, Flynn. So much.'

He swung his head around, capturing her mouth. She swayed and he held her tight, then lifted his head, drawing back a fraction and helping her into the carriage.

'You make me the happiest man in the world.'

Then he was beside her and they were moving, the old town a blur of quaint buildings and upturned faces.

Half an hour later he carried her over the threshold of a suite in a gracious hotel. Ava scanned the luxurious furnishings as Flynn kicked the door shut and strode across the room, still holding her.

She revelled in his display of macho strength. Once free of her father's machinations, she'd fiercely guarded herself from take-charge men. From men, period, except for the odd casual date. But with Flynn the *Me Tarzan, you Jane* show of domination excited rather than repelled her. Who'd have thought it?

Her gaze caught on a lavish buffet on the elegant dining table.

'Are we expecting guests?' Ava frowned.

He halted and she felt his heartbeat slam against his ribs where he held her. She pressed her palm to his chest, loving the feel of him, relishing the fact that, for all his power, he was as affected as she.

'Absolutely not! Why?'

She waved towards the antique table and he smiled, resuming his stride.

'That's our wedding breakfast.'

'But there's enough for an army.'

He slanted a glance at her that made a flock of butterflies in her stomach suddenly take flight.

'The chef probably thought we'd need to keep up our strength.'

On those words they passed into a bedroom dominated by a massive four-poster bed, its covers turned down and its long, filmy curtains drawn back with ties of gold damask. The rich scent of roses wafted from crystal vases on the mantelpiece and pale petals were scattered across the sheets. Beside the bed a bottle nestled in a silver wine cooler.

The scene might have been a cliché, but from her vantage point in Flynn's embrace it looked wonderful. It meant so much that he'd pulled out all the stops to make today romantic and special.

'Oh, Flynn. This is gorgeous. Thank you.'

'It's my pleasure, believe me.' He pressed a kiss to her hair and settled her on the bed. Then he turned to lift the bottle from its bucket.

Used to her father's ostentatious displays of wealth, Ava nevertheless felt her eyes widen. The label belonged to a wine she'd heard of, never seen. It was famed as much for its exclusiveness as its quality. Few could afford it. Michael Cavendish would have given his eye teeth to taste it—more, to serve it to the people he'd always aimed to impress. Imagine his chagrin if he'd been alive to see the under-gardener's son drinking it. The idea made her smile.

'To us.'

The bed sank as Flynn sat beside her and passed her a glass of golden wine.

Ava took it, relieved to banish thoughts of her father. Warmth flooded her as Flynn's hand brushed hers and she sank sideways a little, coming up against him.

'To us.'

Holding his eyes, she lifted the glass and sipped. Luscious rich fruit danced on her tongue, then slid down her throat.

'That's amazing,' she whispered, understanding why connoisseurs raved about it.

But far more amazing was the way Flynn made her feel.

She took another drink, savouring the deliciousness, then held out her glass. 'But it's not wine I want.'

Light flared in those dark eyes as he put their glasses on the table.

'What *do* you want, Ava?' His voice scraped softly, like fingers trawling through thick fur. She felt it as a ripple down her back.

'You.' Her hands went to his tie, dealing with the knot, then pulling it undone. Beneath her hands heat radiated up. 'Only you.' The tie arced through the air as she tossed it away and reached for his top button.

'Since you ask so nicely, Mrs Marshall...'

He shrugged out of his jacket and dropped it to the floor, but the gleam in his eyes told her the humour was camouflage. His expression was hungry. He looked as if he wanted to devour her whole. It made her jittery, despite her excitement.

That had to be first-time nerves. There was nothing to worry about. Flynn loved her as she loved him. It was simply that for the first time he'd allowed her to glimpse the intensity of what he felt. Not possessiveness, but love, she assured herself.

Seconds later his shirt was gone and Ava sucked in a breath at his sculpted perfection.

Leanly built, Flynn nevertheless had muscles in all the right places. The symmetry of his body, the ripple of strength in his pectorals and tight abs drew her. She edged closer, that clean outdoor scent tickling her nostrils.

She lifted her palms to his chest, feeling soft hair tickle, heat spreading from his flesh to hers. Runnels of sensation shot up her arms and then down through her body, to her breasts, her pelvis and belly. Her breath was cut short and shallow, loud in the silence.

'*Now*, Flynn. I need you.' She shifted closer, twisting to raise one leg over him. She wanted to consummate this desire that had built to scorching point.

'Whoa.' He leaned back, his hand at her waist, holding her still. 'Wait a minute.'

She frowned. 'I don't want to wait. I want you now.'

She pressed a kiss to the hot flesh of his chest. He tasted of spice and salt and she wanted more. Drawing in a quick breath, she licked along his collarbone, triumph rising as he shuddered, his hands tightening around her.

An instant later she was lying on the bed with him rising over her.

Ava smiled. *Yes!* She shifted, her thighs opening, her breath quickening.

Flynn shook his head. 'Let me do this right.'

Abruptly he was sitting back, the delicious body contact gone.

Bemused, she stared as he lifted her hand, holding it and flicking the first button at her wrist undone.

'What are you doing?'

'Seducing my bride.' His smile was tight.

'You don't need to seduce me! I'm already seduced.' Her heart thudded nineteen to the dozen. All she wanted was Flynn.

She tried to sit up but he pushed her gently back onto the cushioning mattress. The scent of roses surrounded her.

'Let me do this for you, Ava. I want your first time to be perfect, not over before it begins.'

How could she resist when it was Flynn asking? Flynn's eyes holding her captive? Flynn denying himself so he could give her what he thought she needed?

She felt her sleeve loosen as another button flicked open. Flynn dipped his head and pressed a kiss to the spot. Another button, another kiss, and another and another. Such simple caresses surely shouldn't be so devastating. Yet with each kiss a buzz of excitement shot between her legs, making her ache.

'Do you know how many buttons there are on this dress?' she croaked. 'Dozens!'

'And I'm looking forward to every single one.'

He nuzzled the soft flesh at the underside of her arm and a shiver ripped through her.

By the time he'd finished both sleeves Ava was flushed with arousal. His eyes were hooded as he took her hands in his and pulled her up to sit beside him. *At last!*

His lips on hers made her sigh. Relief and anticipation swamped her. She couldn't take much more of his slow seduction. Already she was trembling at the devastating impact of his tender assault.

The kiss ended and Flynn shifted, shucking his shoes and, before she could protest, moving to sit behind her, his long legs encasing hers. His heat wrapped her, from his torso at her back, his arms around her. Something hard nudged the base of her spine. She shifted, feeling his erection through the layers of cloth between them.

Ava's eyelids fluttered as one large hand skimmed the lace of her bodice. She arched into his touch and was rewarded when his fingers closed around her breast.

Yes! That felt so good. She felt she'd waited a lifetime for Flynn's touch.

At the same time his other hand began dealing with the buttons at her neck, his mouth hot against her nape. Flynn's kisses were different now, quicker, fervid.

She sensed the difference in him—not so in control now. The realisation delighted her.

Ava's mouth curved as she snuggled her bottom back against Flynn's groin, her hands sliding along his powerful thighs. She felt hot muscles, hard as honed steel, and felt his sudden exhalation at her neck.

'Witch!'

Thrilled, she felt the surge of her feminine power, for all Flynn's take-charge attitude.

'It's your own fault for taking so long with those buttons.' If she'd had her way she'd have kept the dress on, so desperate was she.

But as the back of the bodice flopped open and Flynn shifted, lifting the dress up, Ava couldn't help but appreciate his tender care. He knew it was her first time and wanted it to be just right.

In her heart she knew making love with Flynn would be perfect however they did it. She loved him so much.

Arms in the air, she let him drag the gown away, leaving her in lacy knickers and strapless bra. Her shoes were already tumbled on the carpet.

Flynn laid her dress over a chair. She missed his heat. But when he turned back the way he surveyed her almost made her want to cover herself. That untamed side of him had surfaced, making her both nervous and triumphant. Her damp hands clenched as she returned his hungry stare.

Deliberately she lifted one hand to the catch of her bra and snapped it undone. Her breasts jiggled free, the air caressing them as the bra fell away.

She watched Flynn's chest rise and fall as a groan sighed out of him.

'Have you finished playing games?' she whispered, in a voice she barely recognised.

He stepped back to the bed, towering over her, the bulge in his trousers enormous, his muscled body sheened with heat.

'This is no game, Ava. You're mine now.'

His low growl hummed with a possessiveness that once would have scared her. Now she was thrilled by it. She was his and he was hers.

One stride and he was pushing her back onto the bed, lifting her higher so she lay full length. Then he was beside her, over her, the weight of one solid thigh pinning her legs, his groin hot at her hip.

Flynn's mouth swooped on hers, enticing, demanding, driving her crazy, and she grabbed his shoulders, desperate. His hand slid across her bare stomach and she sighed into his mouth. *At last!* She shimmied her hips, ready to help him drag her knickers off. Instead his hand arrowed beneath them, zeroing straight beneath the lace to the nub of her desire.

Ava gasped and clung to his broad shoulders as long fingers circled, delved and circled again. Wildfire raced through her, tongues of flame licking everywhere.

Her hips rose needily as with one expert stroke, then another, he built a crescendo of sensation. It crested in seconds, a fiery maelstrom that blasted through her, leaving her quaking in ecstasy.

Dazed, Ava stared into Flynn's face, now tight with restraint. His features looked moulded from bronze, his eyes molten hot.

Shakily she reached out to cup his jaw, feeling the tension hum through him. She dragged air into oxygen-starved lungs.

'I need you,' she whispered.

He pressed his lips to hers in a kiss so delicate she felt adoration and love and her heart swelled. His feelings were there in every touch, every caress.

'I love you.' Her mouth curved. It felt good to say it out loud. Powerful and precious.

Flynn's eyes looked black as night as he scanned her face, as if committing it to memory.

'Ava.'

Just two syllables, but they were invested with such depth of feeling her throat convulsed from the emotional overload.

His fingers stroked again, gently, and she stiffened, lax muscles suddenly rigid, senses alert. There it was again, that spark of desire flickering anew.

Flynn's mouth tipped up at the corner as her body came to life again.

He didn't give her time to think but slipped down, swirling his tongue around her nipple, then drawing it into his mouth. She'd never felt the like of it. She grabbed his thick black hair, clamping him to her as delight and wonder broke upon her. Each lave of his tongue sent her spiralling further out of control till she couldn't stop the mews of pleasure.

Desperation gave way to relief as he finally skimmed her panties off, pushing her legs apart. She complied with alacrity, more than ready for him.

But instead her new husband slid down further, pushing her knees wide and settling there, where the heat burned brightest.

'Flynn!' Her shocked gasp died when he nuzzled her aroused pulse-point and she almost lifted off the bed.

Eyes wide, she saw him watching her. One slow lick and her breath evaporated. Another and she was rigid with pleasure. But what made the experience so shockingly erotic was Flynn's knowing gaze as he watched the hectic flush spread over her breasts and throat. Her eyes widened and her trembling lips parted in a gasp as another climax broke upon her.

It was so intense she could have sworn she floated free of her body, quivering as wave after wave hit, anchored only by the grip of the man she loved, the man who pleasured her so generously.

Still quivering, Ava was grateful for the comfort of his big body as he moved up the bed and wrapped her close, soothing her with large, calming hands as he pulled her across and over him. Against her ear his heart pounded strong and steady, a contrast to her own wildly hammering pulse. Only his quickened breathing indicated it was difficult for him to take his time. That and his erection, hot against her.

She burrowed in to Flynn, overwhelmed, needing the reassurance of his arms around her.

Finally her pulse slowed to something less than frantic and she nuzzled his collarbone, one weighted hand trawling over his ridged abdomen.

'Thank you, Mr Marshall.' Her voice was husky, not her own. 'That was very…' Words failed her.

'Pleasant?' he murmured against her hair. 'Nice?'

A huff of laughter broke from her still tight throat. 'How about earth-shattering?'

'I'm afraid not, Mrs Marshall.'

His voice caressed like a lingering touch and a tiny shiver rippled across her bare flesh.

'Earth-shattering is in a completely different category. We're working up to that slowly.'

Ava tilted her head, meeting his look. Her heart gave a great thump at the tenderness she saw there.

'I'm not sure I've got the stamina. Or that I'd survive it.'

Flynn's lips curved rakishly. 'You don't know what you're capable of yet.'

His stare sizzled and she was grateful she lay in his arms as every bone in her body melted.

He pressed a kiss to her ear, then nipped the lobe, and something jolted through her. He did it again, and to her amazement her replete body began to re-awaken.

'Allow me to demonstrate.'

The demonstration took some time.

In her wildest fantasies Ava had never imagined loving like this. His care, patience and generosity were phenomenal. Though he seduced her into pleasure, clearly it came at a cost. He was strung taut as a bow, his big body humming with tension, jerking when she raked her fingers over him.

When finally he settled over her, his weight heavy between her spread thighs, Ava was in a haze of wellbeing. Excitement rose at the prospect of Flynn finally easing that hollow ache within.

Ava lifted heavy arms, sliding them around the smooth skin of his sides. She loved his heat and hardness, his warm scent in her nostrils.

'This could hurt a little.' Flynn's voice was tight, the tendons in his neck pronounced.

'I don't care. I just want you. Now, Flynn. Please.'

With a long, slow push he moved. Ava caught her breath at the unfamiliar sensation. So strange and yet so wonderful. Still it went on. There was a moment's pause as she fought for oxygen, striving to absorb the unaccustomed feeling of fullness, then with a grunt of satisfaction he slid home, right to the core of her.

'Okay?' A frown raked his brow.

Ava's pulse pumped hard and fast, her breath was ragged, but she felt her smile widen. 'Marvellous.'

Then there were no more words, just the smooth slide of Flynn's body against hers, starting slowly, almost tentatively, until Ava found the rhythm in her blood and learned to move with it. Their pace picked up, their breaths mingling. Ava's pulse thudded as Flynn's gaze held hers, the stroke of his body in hers drawing her impossibly higher all over again.

Such need, such connection…it was beyond her imaginings.

Wanting to hold him as close as possible, Ava managed to lift her legs. She wrapped them high around his waist, drawing him to her with the last of her strength, and was rewarded with a hoarse gasp of masculine pleasure.

As if she'd released him from restraint Flynn moved faster, harder, taking her somewhere she'd never been before. Then, with a final mighty thrust, he catapulted her into that other world. Rapture engulfed her, overwhelming her senses with pleasure so intense she thought she might die of it.

She heard Flynn call her name, felt the hot release of his orgasm, and sank into oblivion, sated, exhausted, and loved beyond her wildest dreams.

Flynn looked down into her flushed face, at the hint of a smile curving that petal-soft mouth, and felt as if the ground had dropped away beneath him.

His heart plunged, then steadied. His chest pumped like a piston, hammering desperately. He'd passed through fire. Shreds of ecstasy lingered, lending this moment a vibrant, unreal quality that was unfamiliar.

Sex was always good, but this…

He shook his head, trying to gather his thoughts.

Forcing his protesting body to move, he rolled onto his back, clasping Ava so she lay across him, her head on his chest. Of their own volition his hands spread over the hot silk of her skin, so incredibly soft. Untouched till him.

The thought should have made him smile. To be Ava's first lover was an unlooked-for honour. He'd barely been able to believe it when he'd realised how inexperienced she was. Who'd have thought it of Michael Cavendish's daughter?

But Ava was nothing like her father. He wouldn't have married her if she had been.

She was unique.

A virgin till she gave herself to him.

Maybe that was why he felt so odd. Winded, and not just physically from that searing, glorious orgasm and from watching her come apart for him time and again. She'd been so responsive, so innocently wanton, purring like a cat when he stroked her, her eyes wide with shock as he pleasured her so thoroughly.

Why had he?

Sure, he had enough experience to know a satisfied partner made sex all the better. But he'd far surpassed what was necessary. Even inexperienced Ava had known that, urging him to take her as he'd wanted for so long.

He pulled her close, inhaling the perfume of her rose-scented skin. His hands tightened.

Damn! He was hard for her, ready to take her again, though she slumbered, snuggling trustingly as she dozed. His lips thinned. He'd have to wait. She wasn't ready and he didn't want to hurt her.

Flynn told himself that was why he'd taken such care, giving her climax after climax, ensuring she wasn't too tense to enjoy her first time.

But his motivation hadn't been quite so simple. He'd felt an unsettling kernel of discomfort when she'd gazed into his eyes and told him she loved him.

He should have expected it. It wasn't the first time

she'd said it, with that dewy-eyed look of wonder. Yet hearing the words, watching her say them, had battered at him.

Flynn stroked the sinuous curve of her back, enjoying having her here, where she belonged.

She was exactly the right woman for him and he intended to look after her, ensuring she had everything she could possibly want or need, everything she'd once had and lost.

Still her words niggled.

Flynn set his chin. Ava would never regret her decision to marry him. He'd make sure of it.

Yet his determination couldn't quite banish his discomfort. He frowned. He knew beyond all doubt that marrying Ava was right. It had been the sensible, logical decision. The best decision for them both.

But in all his analysis he'd missed one thing—the way he'd feel when Ava looked at him with stars in her eyes and said she loved him.

Could it be...? Was it possible that *guilt* had motivated him to provide such a fancifully romantic wedding? To make her wedding night everything and more that a blushing bride could wish?

Guilt because it wasn't love that had led him to marry her.

CHAPTER SIX

AVA SMOTHERED A GASP as Flynn opened the apartment's front door. Even from the entrance its view across London was spectacular. She'd expected something special after he'd ushered her into a sleek Aston Martin at Heathrow, and when he'd led her to the private lift in this prestige residential block. But still…

'You didn't tell me—'

Powerful arms closed around her, sweeping her up against Flynn's chest. He made her feel delicate, cosseted. Ava enjoyed the unfamiliar sensation of being fussed over. She'd never been cosseted in her life.

Her world was full of firsts with Flynn. Even dreams seemed possible.

Ava wrapped her arms around his neck, pressing a kiss to his bronzed throat. She loved the way the pulse-point there quickened when they made love. It proved that, despite Flynn's constant restraint, his insistence on treating her like some dainty princess, he was as aroused as she.

'Welcome to my home, Mrs Marshall. *Our* home, until we find somewhere together.'

He carried her into the penthouse, nudging the door shut behind them, and her heart gave a tiny jump of excitement. This was the first day of the rest of her life. A life she and Flynn would share.

'Thank you, Mr Marshall.' She planted another kiss on his throat, inhaling his unique fresh scent.

'What didn't I tell you?'

Still he didn't put her down, but strode into an enormous sitting room with expansive views. Ava wondered if he enjoyed holding her as much as she liked being held. In Prague he'd carried her to the bath when they'd woken after making love. A bath scented with rose petals! Then he'd carried her back to bed, as if concerned walking would be too taxing for her after that bone-melting initiation into love-making.

'You didn't warn me you're rich as Croesus.' She kept her tone light, ignoring a frisson of disquiet.

It wasn't that she didn't like luxury. She'd been born to privilege. But she'd seen how the desire for wealth could corrupt people. She shivered and he clasped her closer.

She'd rather have her busy, average life with its simple pleasures than move back into that cold, harsh world where money ruled.

'I prefer to call myself comfortable.'

He lowered her to her feet and Ava sank back against him. Being in Flynn's arms made her feel complete, as if all was well with the world.

What a change from the past, when she'd avoided men who'd tried to get too close.

Ava let her head rest on his shoulder as she scanned the room's designer-perfect luxury. She was beginning to realise how much her life might change with Flynn. She'd altered since she met him—love did that. But now there was his lifestyle to adjust to too.

'If that painting is what I think it is...' she peered, eyes widening, at the masterpiece on the far wall '..."comfortable" is an understatement.'

Flynn shrugged. 'It's just a painting.'

'*Just* a painting?'

Through her brother Rupert she had an interest in art. This work was an iconic piece of French Impressionism. A piece any gallery would proudly hang. She loved its colour and vibrant sense of light. Yet Flynn saw *just a painting*?

'It looks good there, don't you think?'

Ava expected to see pleasure or pride in his face. Instead his expression was dispassionate.

She frowned. Why buy a work of art unless you had a passion for it?

'You bought it to fit the room?' It seemed excessive, spending a fortune on a single piece just to make the room look right.

Flynn shrugged. 'It was a good investment.'

Ava stared from the painting to him. It was true. He felt no connection with the work. He looked as if he was calculating the cost-benefit ratio of buying this work over some other.

A cool finger of memory traced her spine.

When she was tiny a truckload of books had been delivered to the Hall. Given her love of picture books, she'd been thrilled as pallet after pallet of books had been unloaded, only to be disappointed when she'd been ordered to keep away. Those serious-looking hardbacks weren't for *reading*, she'd been informed. Her father had bought them in bulk to fill the half-empty shelves in the old library and he didn't want sticky little fingers on them.

She hadn't understood till years later that he'd done it so the room, and by association he, could look suitably impressive. For what was a commercial mogul without his den? Or an aristocrat, even if only by marriage, without his ancient country estate and an impressive library?

'Show me the rest of the place?'

Suddenly Ava was eager to leave this beautiful room, with its unsettling sense of being a showpiece instead of a home. Besides, exploring would give her a chance to discover more about Flynn. She longed to uncover clues to the man she'd married. Though she knew the important things, she was still a stranger to his everyday world.

Ava smiled as he threaded his fingers through hers. Who cared about luxury when there were simple pleasures like this to enjoy?

'If you keep looking at me like that...' his voice was gruff '...we'll go straight to the bedroom and stay there.'

'Well...' She pretended to consider, her insides turning molten in anticipation. 'We could finish our tour in the bedroom.'

A spark ignited in his eyes and she watched that telltale pulse in his throat flicker.

'Or we could stay here.' Her gaze lingered on a leather sofa long enough to take even Flynn's tall form. Excitement buzzed. In the two days they'd been married they'd never made love outside a bed. What would it be like, lying there brazenly naked with Flynn?

'Except my housekeeper won't yet have left for the day.'

Flynn's words punctured Ava's erotic fantasy. 'You have a housekeeper?'

'I don't look after all this myself.'

Of course not. She should have realised. But she hadn't been thinking about anything except Flynn.

'Don't worry.' He leaned close. 'She doesn't live in. We'll have plenty of privacy.'

Ava nodded and swallowed down the knot of tension that had risen. She had no reason to feel unnerved. Having daily help wasn't like living at Frayne Hall, with its retinue of staff. Her father had insisted on having people on tap to do his bidding, including Flynn's parents—his mother in the kitchen and his father in the grounds.

But Ava couldn't repress regret. She'd made a point of leaving that behind her, throwing off the shackles of her family's way of life.

'Come on. There's a lot to see.'

The apartment was magnificent—decorated in a style that screamed expense. Everything from the giant media room to the rooftop pool, spa and sauna was designed for maximum enjoyment. The facilities were state-of-the-art, right down to the sophisticated electronic environment controls in each room.

Yet Ava couldn't shift a sense of unease. Each room was perfect, a showpiece worthy of a design magazine. But none, not even the kitchen, seemed homelike.

The views were spectacular, the finishes gorgeous,

but her minuscule kitchen with its sunshine-yellow curtains and collection of quirky novelty teapots had far more character and warmth.

'Where do you spend most of your time?' she asked as Flynn led her through another sumptuous sitting room in neutral tones to a dining room that seated twenty.

'Me?' His brows lifted. 'The master suite, I suppose. I work long hours and only come home to sleep.'

'Ah. I see.' No wonder the apartment felt more like a glamorous hotel than a home.

He cupped her face, his touch warm. 'Though that will change.' His voice took on that husky, sensual quality that set ribbons of heat unfurling through her. 'Sleep is overrated.'

Ava adored it when Flynn looked at her like that, as if nothing mattered but what they shared. She reached up and palmed his jaw, enjoying the scrape of bristles against her skin and the tantalising hint of the outdoors that seemed to be a scent innate to him.

'Perhaps it's time you showed me the master suite.'

For answer, he shepherded her past a sleek office and a well-equipped gym into a vast bedroom.

The floor was acres of polished wood. Huge windows looked on to the City of London. The walls were just a shade on the chic side of steel-grey, and accents of black and white turned the room into a statement of designer elegance, perfect and impersonal.

Ava's gaze swept around, seeking bookcases, photos, mementoes. But there was nothing personal on display. Not even a book on the bedside table.

She frowned. She'd expected *something*. This felt curiously empty. As if Flynn had no life here at all.

The thought struck that perhaps he lived for his work. But that didn't tally with the man she'd fallen in love with in Paris and Prague. There had to be another explanation.

Slowly she turned, taking in the crisp perfection of the wide bed, the cool, bordering on cold colours, the lack of softness. She stopped, her breath jamming in her chest then expelling in an audible whoosh. Her pulse racketed.

On the far side of the room, facing the bed, was a huge oil painting—the one thing in this pristine room not stylishly contemporary. It was rich and unashamedly beautiful, the ornate gilt frame enhancing rather than detracting from the wash of golden light in the scene.

Ava stepped closer, then stopped, her heart pumping hard against her ribs. She felt strangely wobbly.

'My father got rid of this years ago.'

Michael Cavendish had disdained the picture, despite the money spent on its commission—or not spent, if the artist was to be believed. He'd maintained her father had reneged on payment and threatened court action.

Ava didn't know what had happened in the end— just that after one short week in Frayne Hall the painting had been sent back and her father had growled about it for months. He'd never taken it well when he didn't get precisely what he wanted.

Ava's sympathies had been with the artist. She'd have bet her then empty purse he hadn't won his battle for compensation. Her father had been a master at manipulating deals to suit himself.

'How did you find it?'

'I sourced it at an auction.'

She moved closer, mesmerised by what the artist had captured. Frayne Hall, lit by early-morning light, glowed like a dream of bucolic England. Even the mock gothic towers, added in the nineteenth century, complemented rather than mocked the much older bones of the building. Light glinted off huge mullioned windows and the scene looked idyllic.

Frayne Hall as it should have been, Ava thought.

Anyone intimate with family life inside its mellow stone walls ten years ago would have painted a very different picture. There should at least have been storm clouds and lightning tearing open the sky.

Yet even with rancid memories surfacing Ava was drawn. Her family might have been rotten at the core, but the Hall was a beautiful old place. Generations of her mother's family had been born, had loved and died under its roof. Maybe that was why she felt this connection to it, despite the memories time hadn't erased.

'You like it?' Flynn spoke from just behind her.

Ava nodded, surprising herself. 'I do. It looks...'

She couldn't think of the word. Appealing...solid. As if her father's reign there had been the merest blip, soon forgotten. As if the old place had survived and moved on.

She wished she were as unmarked by that time as the old house.

'I'm glad you approve.'

She swung round, reading satisfaction on Flynn's face.

'You bought it for *me*?'

Nothing would surprise her. Not after the lengths Flynn had gone to to make their wedding a romantic dream. Her mind boggled at the cost and organisation required to arrange everything so speedily and exquisitely.

Obviously Flynn didn't know how much she'd hated life at Frayne Hall. The Cavendishes had been experts at projecting the perfect family image, even in front of servants. Of course some must have guessed, but perhaps not Flynn's mother, who'd spent her time in the kitchen, or his dad who'd worked out-doors.

Or maybe his mother had kept those details from her son. Ava remembered Mrs Marshall's quiet kind-ness whenever as a child she'd escaped to Frayne Hall's cavernous kitchen. Ava had always been drawn to her, with her comfortable air of quiet competence and understanding.

'Flynn?'

'I thought you might like it,' he said at last.

'I'm surprised Rupert didn't mention seeing it in a sale catalogue. He's interested in the market.' As an artist, Rupe kept abreast of what was selling.

Flynn took a moment to answer. 'Actually, I saw it some years ago and...' He shrugged. 'It appealed.'

Ava regarded him curiously. 'Appealed to you enough to hang it on your bedroom wall?'

Something bristled, some sixth sense, prickling her skin. Instinct told her she was missing something. What were the chances a painting of her old home, no matter how beautifully executed, should so ap-peal to Flynn?

Then realisation hit. 'Of course. The estate was your childhood home too. Lots of happy memories for you there.'

Ava imagined him spending long, lazy summer days exploring the grounds, enjoying freedoms she'd rarely been permitted. He'd run wild in the forest, always up to no good, her father had said. But Ava had envied him even when he'd had to spend time helping his dad, maintaining the pristine lawns and formal gardens.

Flynn's mouth hooked up at the corner in a smile that wasn't a smile. 'Lots of memories, certainly.'

Ava tilted her head, trying to place that look, that tone. It wasn't happiness.

'Flynn?' She moved closer, grasping his arm. Beneath his jacket his bicep was taut. 'What's wrong?'

Was it crazy to imagine shadows in those dark eyes?

He stared down at her and Ava had the strangest sensation that she looked into a stranger's gaze. Then he shrugged.

'Nothing's wrong. Everything's perfect.' He looked at the painting and this time his smile was genuine.

'But there was something, wasn't there?' If something bothered Flynn she wanted to know. How could she support him if she didn't understand? Ava stroked her hand through his too short hair, its plush softness inviting.

He turned to her again, his hand capturing hers.

He pressed her palm to his lips, kissing her there, making heat pool in her belly.

'My memories of Frayne Hall aren't all good, that's all.'

'Of course.' Ava should have realised. 'Your father...'

Flynn nodded. 'He died the Christmas I turned sixteen.'

'That's something we have in common. My mother died when I was sixteen. But you'd moved away by then.'

'I still came back.'

It was Ava's turn to nod. Flynn had always returned to visit his mother. She'd envied them their closeness, the love they'd obviously shared. 'Your mother was always so pleased to have you home.'

The Marshalls' relationship had reinforced all that had been wrong with her family. When they'd got together it had been to impress her father's VIP 'friends' and associates.

For a week before the glittering winter ball Michael Cavendish had always hosted an open house for those he wanted to impress. Every member of the family had to be at their best, projecting the perfect image—or face the consequences.

She remembered the year Rupe, then just a kid, had caught a stomach bug and vomited over the polished shoes of a very important banker. Their father had made his life hell for weeks.

Worse was an earlier memory, from a night when she'd sneaked out of bed to catch a glimpse of the ball. Ava had seen her mother, soignée and perfect in silk and pearls, but her smile had been wrong as she'd talked with one of her husband's friends. The man had stood too close, his hands moving over her in a way little Ava had known wasn't right. But Michael Cavendish, right beside them, pretended not to notice.

The scene had scared Ava. For she'd seen fear in her mother's eyes and known something was badly wrong.

It was only years later that she'd understood.

Her heart hammered.

What would have happened the night of that last ball if Flynn hadn't come back to visit his mother? If it hadn't been he who'd found Ava in her wrecked car? She shuddered, old fears crowding.

'Ava?' Flynn wrapped his other arm around her, holding her close. 'What is it?'

She sank into his heat, loving the feeling of safety Flynn gave her. After years of looking after herself it was amazing how wonderful it felt to lean on someone else just a little. To know he loved her.

'Nothing important.' When his frown didn't shift

she said, 'Not all *my* memories of the Hall are good either. But that doesn't matter now.'

Should she unburden herself about her father, or that last fraught night at the Hall? Maybe Flynn had some inkling her family hadn't been all her father had wanted it to appear. But her father was dead and the past with him. He couldn't hurt her now. She'd worked so hard to put all that behind her and look forward. Surely the past was better buried—especially now, when she was so happy? She didn't want anything to ruin this.

'You're trembling.' Flynn's hold tightened.

'Maybe you could soothe me.' Ava pressed closer, deliberately shifting against his groin.

His crooked smile ignited now familiar fire.

'How would you like to be soothed?' His voice was hot chocolate laced with brandy, his eyes heavy-lidded.

'Make love to me.'

Ava stood on tiptoe, planting her mouth on his, slicking her tongue along his lips till he opened and let her in. She sighed at the blissful sense of rightness she always felt when they kissed.

Flynn hugged her close and she felt his body's instant response. She smiled against his mouth.

'I want you, Flynn. Now.'

Eagerly she lifted one leg up around his hip and his

hand clamped her there. Desire slammed into her. A second later his other hand was hauling up her other leg, holding her off the ground, her feminine heat centred against his erection. She locked her ankles behind him, revelling in his easy strength.

'Yes...'

It was a triumphant hiss. She needed him *now*. The blast of arousal was too strong to ignore or to wait. Ava dragged his mouth to hers, kissing him as if it had been a lifetime, not mere hours since they'd made love.

Flynn made her insatiable. For the fireworks and the rockets. But also for that sense of oneness she'd only ever experienced with him—the knowledge that she shared herself, body and soul, with the one man in the world she'd ever love. The one man who loved her for herself.

She kissed him with all the pent-up passion of a woman who'd spent a lifetime hiding her feelings—a woman only now learning to glory in the freedom to love and be loved.

Flynn groaned, his fingers digging into her. She felt the wall at her back as he used it to leverage her into a better position. She was caught between it and him, unable and not wanting to move as desire peaked.

His kiss turned ferocious, devouring her, and she

gloried in it. To be so desired was incredibly exciting. It made her feel powerful.

One big hand slid up her thigh, roughly pushing her skirt higher, baring her. Through her laboured breathing she heard something tear and shivered voluptuously.

'Yes. Like that.' She arched her head back as his mouth dipped to her throat and all her senses sang. There was something incredibly arousing about Flynn's sheer strength and hunger. She needed him hard and fast, just the two of them and the raw passion they shared.

'Take me here. Like this.'

Flynn dragged his mouth away with a final scrape of teeth on flesh that made her quiver deep in her womb. Then eyes like fathomless night met hers. His mouth was open, dragging in air, and she knew he saw the hectic colour in her face, the hungry glitter in her eyes.

It took a second for her to realise his hands had stopped their upward progress. That he stood unmoving, merely supporting her as she rubbed herself against him.

'Flynn?'

'Let's do this properly.' He swung her around, away from the wall, holding her to him as he paced to the bed.

'Properly?' She was at fever-pitch.

Then she felt the mattress at her back as he lowered her gently onto the bed. She clung, trying to draw him down, but he broke her hold to stand over her.

'Flynn! I need you!' Outrage and loss made her voice uneven. She felt bereft.

'Soon.' He tore his shirt off to reveal that magnificent torso she routinely used as a pillow.

Some of her distress evaporated as he shucked his shoes and undid his belt. But that didn't diminish her urgency. Need was a living force, writhing within her.

'Why did you stop?'

'Because I want it to be good for you.'

He came down onto the bed, reaching for her breast. His touch was gentle, the merest brush of fingertips across her nipple through her top, yet she was wound so tight it made her arch almost off the bed.

'It was good for me before.' She clutched him to her, turning her body into his.

'But this will be better. Trust me.'

He dipped his head and Ava was lost.

Later, much later, Ava lay naked against him. Flynn had brought her to climax several times. He'd been tender and clever and passionate and her body was so deliciously sated she felt like she'd never move again.

Her husband was a wonderful, generous lover, always ensuring she was satisfied. Her heart thudded. More than satisfied.

She rubbed her hand over the smooth curve of his shoulder and nuzzled closer, drawing in the man musk scent of his hot skin.

She was incredibly lucky.

So why did she feel that little niggle of—no, not discontent—curiosity, maybe? It wasn't that she wanted rough sex. But earlier, when she'd felt the rising force of carnal need between them, when she'd thought for once Flynn would give in to that primitive urge and take her with all the force and hunger she'd felt in him...

She sighed. There'd been something elemental about it...so unrestrained.

Ava skimmed her fingers down his arm and he grunted, shifting beneath her, his breathing deep and even.

The trouble was she was still so inexperienced at sex. She had nothing to compare this with. Making love with Flynn was magnificent, rapturous and fulfilling. But those couple of times when she'd felt him teeter on the brink of control had been utterly thrilling. She couldn't help but wonder what would have happened if he hadn't pulled back. If he hadn't treated her like some porcelain princess who needed gentle handling.

Was Flynn afraid she couldn't cope with the real man? The man behind the charm and sophistication?

If only he knew. That was the man she'd fallen in love with—the one whose laughter was infectious. The one whose passion convinced her she was the one woman in the world for him.

'I love you,' she murmured against his chest.

He didn't answer.

He must be asleep.

CHAPTER SEVEN

'So soon?' Ava tried to keep the discontent from her voice. She wasn't unreasonable. She knew Flynn had pushed aside a lot of work to be with her in Prague. But still… 'We only got back last night.'

He shrugged and tucked into the Eggs Benedict the housekeeper had supplied.

That was another thing. Ava had planned to make them both a special breakfast. She'd imagined carrying it into the bedroom and waking Flynn, feeding him fruit and French toast, spending the morning making love.

But she'd been so exhausted she hadn't even heard Flynn get up. Now he was dressed in a dark suit, suave and dangerously sexy, the epitome of the corporate predator, while she hugged a robe to her breasts and her hair was a morning-after mess.

'It can't be helped. I've got meetings all day.'

His gaze meshed with hers and Ava felt that familiar melting. She sank into the chair beside him, shifting his newspaper. Even after a night spent more often making love than asleep, he reduced her to mush with a look.

She shoved her hair from her face and smiled. She wasn't a morning person, and her plans for a sinfully lazy start to the day were wrecked, but she had no cause to complain.

'You look good enough to eat,' she murmured, pressing a kiss to Flynn's lean cheek. 'You smell good too.'

She reached across to run her fingers through his hair.

'Watch out!' Flynn reared back as something clattered on the table.

Ava looked down. She'd knocked over his coffee. A stain spread across the linen cloth.

'Sorry.' She dabbed it with a napkin before it dribbled off the table. 'Did any spill on you?' She eyed his tailored trousers.

'Please—let me, madam.' It was Sandra, the housekeeper, appearing out of nowhere, whipping things off the table.

Ava sat back, realising there was coffee running down the sleeve of her robe. Hastily she tucked it up so it couldn't drip on Flynn.

Moments later Sandra had efficiently replaced the tablecloth, topped up Flynn's coffee and headed out through the door, her arms full of the stained cloth.

'Sorry about that.' Ava smiled at Flynn as she re-tied her robe that kept slipping open. 'I got a little carried away.'

'No harm done.' He reached for the coffeepot. 'Would you like some?'

'Yes, please. I function better after coffee. I'm not so good in the morning.' She waited for him to make some bantering comment—perhaps a reference to the fact that they'd both been wide awake, making love as the sun came up, but he said nothing.

'Here you are.' Flynn slid a cup to her. His smile was perfunctory rather than warm.

'Flynn? I didn't spill any on your suit, did I?'

'No, it's fine.' He picked up his coffee and sipped, his eyes flicking to the financial pages.

Ava stilled in the act of reaching for her cup. Silly, but she felt as if she'd been dismissed. She opened her mouth, then realised she was about to apologise again and snapped it shut.

'So, you have a busy day lined up?'

Ebony eyes met hers again and she relaxed a frac-tion as familiar heat bored into her. There it was again, that connection. She smiled, happiness surg-ing at the simple joy of being here, with her man.

Flynn nodded and looked back at the newspaper.

Ava's smile faded.

'Yes, meetings all day, making up for the appointments I shifted last week. You'll be busy too.'

'Absolutely.'

She'd go to her flat and begin packing. Moving out would take some organisation. Plus she needed work clothes. It was back to the office tomorrow.

'We're going to a dinner tonight and I'd like you to find something gorgeous to wear.'

'I'm sure I'll find something in my wardrobe.' She leaned forward. 'Where are we going?'

Flynn was an expert at finding secluded romantic restaurants.

He shook his head, his gaze travelling over her silky floral robe. 'No, buy something new.' At her questioning look he added, 'Something formal. Something head-turning.'

His expression as he surveyed her, from the hand clutching her loose robe to the froth of untamed hair clouding around her head, wasn't exactly approving. His eyes were unreadable, curiously blank.

Out of nowhere doubt stabbed. A sliver of remembrance. Of her father's glare when she'd let him down by appearing anything less than perfect.

She shoved the thought aside. Flynn wasn't glaring—just looking.

'I have a formal gown. I wore it to a charity gala I organised.'

Flynn shook his head. 'Buy yourself something brand-new. Something no one has seen. No need to worry about the cost. Here.' He fished out his wallet and withdrew a credit card. 'This is for you.'

Ava picked it up, staring at the sleek platinum card. *Ava Marshall.* It was the first time she'd seen her new name.

Despite his teasing use of her married name in private, she and Flynn hadn't discussed whether she'd keep her surname. Funny that he'd taken it for granted that she'd take his. Was he a traditionalist after all?

Not that it bothered her. Her father had changed *his* name to Cavendish before she was born because it had sounded more upmarket than plain old Cooper. He'd been determined to shake off his working class roots and become a high-flyer financially and socially. He'd been meticulous in ensuring he and his family projected an image of old wealth and class, no matter how fake. Marrying her upper-class mother had been one more crucial step on his upward path.

Ava would far rather share Flynn's name than use a construct of her father's.

'Thank you.' She put the card down. 'But I have my own money.'

They'd have to discuss that. She wasn't naïve enough to think her modest salary working for a children's charity would cover half their joint expenses. But it went against the grain to splurge on Flynn's money. It was one thing to let him shower her with a romantic wedding, but now they were back in the real world and Ava was always meticulous about paying her way.

Flynn's hand clamped hers to the table, the card caught beneath it.

'Keep it, Ava. Use it.' His gaze was serious. 'I want you to look spectacular tonight. In fact, buy several outfits. We'll be out and about a lot.' He paused and after a moment a smile skated across his lips. 'No point draining your savings to impress my associates.'

'It's a business dinner?'

Stupid to feel disappointed that it wasn't a romantic meal for two. She knew Flynn had built his business from nothing. She was proud of the success he'd achieved and intended to support him.

He stroked her hand, sending a shiver of awareness scudding through her.

He leaned in, his breath warm against her ear. 'We'll have plenty of time to be alone afterwards.'

His other hand brushed her lips, his thumb tugging at her bottom lip till her mouth opened on a sigh. Then his lips were there, expertly coaxing, drawing a response that made her toes curl and her blood sizzle.

When Flynn pulled back his eyes gleamed and Ava's breath came in short, choppy gasps.

'You make me want...' His gaze seared and her pulse leapt.

It was still early. Far too early for him to go to the office. But already he was pulling away.

'What do I make you want, Flynn?'

His slow smile was rapacious. He really did look like a corporate raider, with his elegant bespoke clothes and ruthless expression. His gaze dropped to her décolletage and she felt herself flush. Given half a chance she'd climb onto his lap and rip away every elegant, hand-stitched inch of clothing.

'Later, Mrs Marshall.'

His hand slid from hers and the spell broke. He reached for his phone, glanced at the latest message, then pocketed it.

'I have to go.'

'But it's not even eight.' Ava knew she sounded needy—worse, whiny—but she couldn't switch off as Flynn did. How did he *do* that?

'My first meeting is in fifteen minutes.'

Already he was standing, reaching for his jacket. 'So, you'll get a dress? Something glamorous?'

'If that's what you want.' Her voice held a trace of doubt.

It had been years since she'd done glamorous.

Since leaving Frayne Hall she'd developed her own style. Her party clothes were fun and bright. They made her feel good. But they weren't showy or sophisticated. It struck her that she'd deliberately shied away from anything that drew too much male attention.

'I want…' He paused, as if sensing her hesitation. 'I want everyone to know how lucky I am to have you. And as tonight's a formal event—'

'Of course. I understand.' Ava stood too, drawing her belt tight. 'I'll make sure I fit in, don't worry.'

She'd make him proud of her.

It was only after he'd kissed her goodbye and left that Ava realised where her thoughts had taken her. That she planned to make Flynn proud of her not by doing something clever or generous or outstanding, but merely by looking glamorous. As if that was what really mattered.

A shadow flitted across her vision, darkening the morning brightness.

No. This wasn't anything like her father's insistence that she always look as if she'd stepped from a fashion magazine. Even as a child she'd been expected to project the image he wanted.

It was natural that Flynn wanted her to look her best.

There was no similarity to the way Michael Cavendish had shown off his beautiful wife and later his daughter to those awful predatory men.

Flynn loved her. He valued her for herself, not as a trophy or—worse—a tool to further his schemes.

Pushing her hair off her face, she grabbed her coffee and headed for the bathroom. She had a lot to do.

'Sorry. Can you repeat that?' Flynn leaned back in his leather swivel chair and scrubbed a hand down his face.

His PA darted him a surprised look.

Ruefully Flynn smiled, though it was more a grimace, each muscle pulled taut and hard. Just like the rest of him. Even after a morning at work arousal weighed his lower body and his skin felt too tight.

'I'm having trouble concentrating.'

His mind kept straying to Ava. Beautiful Ava. With her just out of bed sleepy smile and flushed cheeks, her hair a downy cloud, her lips bare and temptingly kissable. Every time he'd tried to gather his thoughts and concentrate on tonight's dinner, or getting out through the door to the office, he'd been distracted by the creamy flesh revealed when her wrap slid open, the shadowy cleft between her breasts, or the way her nipples stood proud against the fabric. He swallowed hard.

'That's understandable. You're just back from your wedding. You should be with your bride.'

Flynn's steel-haired, ultra-capable PA was watching him like an indulgent mother, as if pleased at his distraction.

For the first time ever he almost regretted his egalitarian work policies. He prided himself on being a model employer—generous, fair, acknowledging and rewarding good staff, always approachable.

Right now he didn't want to be approachable. He didn't want to be understanding. He needed no-nonsense focus.

Having a wife was far more distracting than he'd imagined.

He couldn't allow himself to be distracted.

'Perhaps we should have pushed those meetings back another week.' His PA looked at her schedule. 'There's nothing so urgent that a week would make a difference.'

'No.' Flynn shook his head.

He never let the grass grow beneath his feet. He'd been lucky in his youth to find a mentor who'd seen his promise despite his lack of qualifications, who'd encouraged his potential, teaching and advising till he'd branched out on his own. But everything he had he'd earned. He'd built his business by pursuing every opportunity with absolute determination. By planning carefully and acting decisively. By getting the best out of his people. By working harder than anyone he knew.

He thought of Ava, with the wind blowing her wheat-blonde hair around her face on that boat in Paris, her surprise and delight when she'd looked up and seen him.

Following through that day was one of the best decisions he'd ever made.

Flynn never wasted an opportunity. As a result his property empire spanned Europe and the US's eastern seaboard. His personal fortune grew faster than current trends, and his social standing too.

Satisfaction stirred. He was on the way to having everything he wanted. Even his mum had finally acquiesced and moved into a new house in an exclusive development. No more leaky drains and cold north-facing rooms for her.

'No. The schedule stays as is. In fact, I'd better get on to the German office about that new retail development.' He glanced at his watch—a premium brand only the mega-wealthy could afford. 'Tee up a conference call for five-thirty. Then tomorrow I'll need a briefing on the Paris option.' He checked his diary. 'Block that in for six.'

His PA's rounded eyes told him what she thought

of him working into the evening so soon after his honeymoon.

Flynn met her stare, refusing to feel defensive. Ava wouldn't thank him if he neglected his business and it turned belly-up, as her father's had after he'd died. She wouldn't be left penniless a second time.

He'd learned a lot from Michael Cavendish. He'd detested the man but envied him deeply: a man who'd shored up his wealth, prestige and power, controlling his world rather than letting it control him.

Flynn had been young when he'd learned life's lessons about the value of power, the things Cavendish's money could buy. Like a good education. Like Cavendish's comfortable life instead of Flynn's father's untimely death. Like a family who had time to enjoy life instead of slaving long hours for others just to keep a roof over their heads.

He'd never forgotten those lessons. He wouldn't stop till he had everything Cavendish had had. Wealth, power, respect, security. The ability to keep his family safe.

But he'd do it properly. Not by grinding people into the dirt, ruthlessly taking advantage of those less fortunate or powerful, as Cavendish had.

That would be his ultimate triumph. He scaled the heights but he prided himself on being a far better man. He worked ethically, supporting his workers, spreading the benefits of success. Doing it better than Cavendish. Proving his superiority over the man who'd so badly injured Flynn's family.

Flynn sat back, feeling the familiar drive to succeed stiffen his resolve.

He smiled at his PA. 'And check the progress of that purchase I left in Reynolds' hands. I have important plans for the place. I want it wrapped up this week.'

CHAPTER EIGHT

'THIS IS MY wife Ava. Ava, I'd like you to meet Alexandra and St John Hardwicke.'

Flynn smiled at the older couple, watching the man's eyes widen in appreciation. His wife gave Ava a comprehensive assessment that took in everything from her hair, smoothed back and up in a style that made her look like a young Grace Kelly, to her silvery couture gown and matching stilettos. Her gaze lingered on Ava's massive square-cut Ceylon sapphire ring.

Flynn had been surprised he'd had to work so hard to persuade Ava to accept the engagement ring. Previous lovers would have been in raptures over such expensive, exquisite jewellery.

Ava shook hands. 'I'm pleased to meet you.' Her beautiful cut-glass voice sliced through the hum of conversation around them and her warm smile made them lean close.

'I had no idea you were married, Flynn.'

'We were married quite recently.'

His gaze narrowed at the way Hardwicke stared at

Ava—like a dog sighting a juicy bone. But one look up at Flynn's face and his expression turned bland again.

'Recently?' Alexandra Hardwicke frowned. 'I didn't hear anything about it. Did I miss it? I didn't read a notice in the newspaper.'

Ava put her hand on his arm, the ring flashing in the light from the chandeliers.

Satisfaction thumped in Flynn's chest. *His* ring. *His* wife. He covered her hand with his and was rewarded with a smile that lit him up inside.

'No, there was no notice.' Ava leaned forward, her voice conspiratorial. 'It was a runaway match.'

'Runaway?' Pencilled eyebrows rose.

She nodded. 'Flynn followed me to Prague, where I was holidaying, and swept me off my feet.' Her sidelong glance from under her lashes turned up the heat inside him a notch. 'We were married there.'

Her look wasn't sultry, like some blatant invitations he'd had in the past. But the emotion in Ava's face, the way her eyes shone as she looked at him, was far more potent. His blood sang. His chest expanded, full and heavy, as if he'd absorbed the inner radiance that made Ava glow.

Heat enveloped him. And a sense of excitement, of *rightness* so strong it almost made him forget why he was there—to grease the wheels of his latest negotiation.

'An elopement?' Alexandra Hardwicke moved closer. 'How unorthodox. But how very romantic.' She flashed Flynn a glance that made it clear she didn't think he had a sentimental bone in his body. Obviously she knew his business reputation.

'Tell me more, my dear. Was it just the pair of you at the wedding?'

'That's how we wanted it. Just us.'

Again that dazzling look. Ava in love outshone any beauty he'd ever met.

Flynn shifted his feet, his heart hitting his ribs.

He'd known they'd be perfect together. And yet... such whole-hearted trust, such transparent adoration, was a little unnerving. It was a huge responsibility to be the cause of her happiness.

He'd never been put on a pedestal in his life—not even by his mother.

'You didn't even have family there?'

'No. My brother is in the States right now, and Flynn's mother is visiting relatives in New Zealand.'

Something new flickered deep inside. Guilt? His mother would have been there like a shot to see him marry. But that would have complicated everything. Better for her to absorb the news that he'd married her old boss's daughter in her own time. He'd let nothing interfere with his plans to marry Ava…like probing questions from the person who knew him best.

'When were you married? Recently, you said?'

'Two days ago.'

'Two *days*!' Alexandra Hardwicke's upper-crust voice edged towards a shriek, drawing the attention of others in the vast reception room. Her gaze turned to Flynn, astonishment on her well-bred face. 'But you should be on your honeymoon!'

'Oh, no. It's fine. Really. We had time in Prague together. Besides, I'm due back at work tomorrow.'

'You *work*? What do you do?' The woman drew Ava close. 'Let's leave the men to their business.' Her sharp gaze lifted to Flynn and her husband. 'This dinner is just an elaborate ruse to keep their womenfolk happy while they talk profits and mergers.'

'I'd guessed that,' Ava murmured with a smile, letting herself be drawn away.

Flynn stood poised to step in if Ava showed signs of being overwhelmed by Alexandra Hardwicke. The woman was renowned for her arrogance as much as her nose for profit, despite the fiction that she left business to her husband. Any deal with Hardwicke would need his wife's approval, which was why Flynn and Ava were here tonight. Until now it had been difficult to get close to them.

But with Ava at his side it was all coming together.

Ava, poised and elegant, looked completely at home in the luxurious surrounds of this exclusive business reception and dinner.

Naturally. That was why she was the perfect wife.

Ava had been born to an aristocratic mother who traced her lineage to the Norman Conquest and was connected to a who's who of British aristocracy. Her father, despite his humble beginnings, had created a business empire that had made him the envy of half the people in this room.

Ava fitted in a way Flynn never would. His father had been Romany, viewed with suspicion if not outright hostility despite settling to domesticity and a steady if underpaid job. His mother had spent years working as a cook for people like those milling around him.

'Your wife's a pretty thing,' boomed Hardwicke. 'And not daunted by Alex. Am I right in thinking she's Cavendish's girl?'

'That's right.'

'Then I believe she may be a distant relative of my wife on her mother's side. No wonder she looks familiar. Her mother was a spectacular woman.'

'Not half as spectacular as Ava.'

Glittering like a princess, with her hair piled high and his ring on her finger, she was stunning. Her smile made him feel like a king who'd just been presented with a kingdom.

'Spoken like a besotted bridegroom. I remember the look on my son-in-law's face when he saw our Lucy...'

Hardwicke launched into a reminiscence that Flynn only half listened to. His attention was on Ava. He expelled his breath. No other woman could hold a candle to her.

Her eyes flicked to his and heat drilled through his belly. Then she turned back to the group around her and Flynn was left grappling with the urge to walk over and haul her away. Not because she needed protection but because he wanted her with him.

Because he wanted to be alone with her.

They should be on their honeymoon.

Alexandra Hardwicke's words sounded in his head.

Flynn wanted to be lying on a tropical beach with Ava. Just the pair of them. No people, no interruptions, no clothes.

Shock hammered. Loafing wasn't his style. Nor was leaving his enterprise to manage itself—which was why he'd spent every night before the wedding working till dawn. Some called him driven. He preferred *focused*. He knew what he wanted and he made sure he got it.

Yet to his surprise a romantic retreat seemed curiously alluring.

Ava hadn't reproached him about returning to London so soon after the wedding. Now it struck him he could at least have asked her.

'So, Marshall, you're interested in doing business?'

Flynn dragged his attention to the man before him. It was disturbing how far his thoughts had wandered.

This was why he'd come tonight. His staff had worked hard on this proposal but Hardwicke had been elusive.

'I see mutual benefits. My company usually works alone, as you know.'

Hardwicke nodded.

'But in this case a joint approach would be more profitable. It's a unique opportunity—as I'm sure your people have told you.' Flynn paused and sipped his wine, deliberately delaying.

He wanted Hardwicke on board, but on *his* terms— not with Hardwicke thinking he had him over a barrel. Flynn was the one in control.

His gaze shifted to Ava, smiling at something one of her companions said. Then she murmured something and they laughed.

Gratification rose. She was perfect…already an asset.

'We should schedule some time to discuss your proposition.'

Flynn turned to Hardwicke. 'I know you'll find it worthwhile.'

'Good, good. I'll have someone contact your office.'

'I'll look forward to it. Your company was my first choice of potential partner in the project.'

He repressed a smile as a frown flickered across Hardwicke's forehead at the implication that his company wasn't the *only* potential partner for the massive redevelopment.

Hardwicke played hard to get. He was wary about working with someone who, for all his success, was over a generation younger, a relative newcomer and an outsider. Flynn had been called lots of things, but never part of the establishment.

'It's an interesting proposal.' It was the first time Hardwicke had admitted it. 'Better yet, rather than a formal meeting, I'll speak to Alex. Have you both round for a meal. Give us a chance to know each other better, eh?'

'Perfect.' Flynn permitted himself a smile. 'Ava will enjoy getting better acquainted with your wife.'

Over the hum of the crowd he hadn't missed Alexandra Hardwicke's carrying voice inviting his wife to call her Alex.

'Excellent. Next week—before we head to our country place. We're looking forward to a break from the city.'

'I know what you mean,' said Flynn, the man who'd spent the last fourteen years living in the city. Who, with the exception of his time wooing Ava, didn't have vacations. 'I'm planning to buy a country place myself.'

'You are?' Hardwicke's brows rose but his tone was pleased. 'Perhaps we have more in common than I'd thought. I had you pegged for an urbanite.'

Flynn swallowed a grim smile. Somewhere along the road to success he'd shucked off his country roots. In his youth the locals, especially Ava's father, had shaken their heads, proclaiming him wild, a half-tamed gypsy who'd never amount to anything. Who'd probably be a poacher or, at best, a jobbing gardener, eking out a living with dirt under his nails like his father.

'I'm country born and bred. Like Ava.'

'Really?' Hardwicke raised his hand to attract a passing waiter, ordering two whiskies. 'A rural upbringing is best. Worked for me and Alex. And our children.'

Flynn forbore from remarking that Hardwicke's experience of rural life was living on a luxurious estate passed from generation to generation, while Flynn's was a cramped cottage with no insulation and a leaking roof their miserly landlord had refused to fix.

'Tell me, Flynn. Where are you looking to buy? I could give you some tips.'

The change in Hardwicke was remarkable. Flynn had known Ava would be useful, but he hadn't expected his own transformation from corporate marauder to respectable married man to be quite so instantaneous.

The smile he gave Hardwicke was his first genuine one of the night.

'You were very popular tonight.' Flynn's voice was deep with satisfaction. 'I had to elbow my way through to take you in to dinner.'

In the darkness, Ava allowed herself the luxury of watching Flynn's hands on the wheel of the Aston Martin, imagining them on her. Anticipation shivered through her, drawing her skin tight.

She'd got through the evening by concentrating on what would come after—being alone with Flynn. She longed for him. Not just his touch, but his attention. She wasn't used to sharing him.

'Everyone was friendly.'

News had spread that Flynn was married, and they couldn't wait to see who'd landed such a catch. She hadn't been the subject of such intense speculation in years, and it had dredged up horrible memories of the year she was seventeen and put on display for her father's 'associates' to drool over.

The shiver became a shudder and she rubbed her hands up her arms.

'Cold?' Instantly Flynn adjusted the air-conditioning.

'No, I'm fine.'

And she was. She'd held her own tonight, for the first time in her life truly grateful for her hard-taught lessons in putting on a public face. No one would have guessed she'd rather wax her legs than make small talk with people who were more interested in showing off their self-importance than getting to know her.

'You enjoyed yourself?' He didn't wait for an answer. 'I'm glad. You wowed them.'

Ava congratulated herself on playing her part well. Tonight had been important to him. She'd noticed his long *tête-à-tête* with St John Hardwicke, and the appraising way Alex Hardwicke had regarded the pair of them, as if deciding whether they met her exalted standards. That had made Ava determined to make a success of the night.

'I knew you'd fit in. They're your sort of people— like the ones your family used to invite to those big parties.'

Ava blinked at '*your* sort of people'. She wanted to tell him *her* sort of people didn't judge by the size of your income or the cost of your clothes. Her sort were ordinary, but genuinely caring. Her friends were more at home laughing over a glass of wine and takeaway pizza than glamming it up at some dire society event.

But she held her tongue.

Lots of women would have given their eye teeth to be there tonight, wearing a designer gown and with a huge, gorgeous rock weighing down their hand.

She'd rather have spent the evening in Flynn's apartment, making love.

Ava firmed her lips. She might be a new bride but she couldn't be selfish about sharing him with his business. It was just a shame they hadn't had longer to themselves before the real world interrupted.

Her hand strayed to his thigh, feeling the heavy bunch of muscle as he shifted gear. In the dark she heard the soft intake of his breath. Her heartbeat pattered faster.

'Did *you* enjoy yourself?' she asked.

'Not as much as I'm going to,' he said, in a voice halfway between a caress and a growl. 'I thought dinner would never end.'

Ava laughed, delight rising. 'Tomorrow I thought we'd have a romantic dinner at home.'

She'd been planning it all day. She'd wear her favourite trousers and the gauzy top in swirls of blue and purple she'd bought today, while shopping for the formal gown. It was more fun than a full-length dress, and sexy too.

Did she have the nerve to wear it without the camisole that kept it decent? She imagined Flynn's reaction and wondered with a shimmy of excitement if they'd make it to the dinner table.

'I'm afraid that's not possible. I've got late meetings the next two nights, catching up on work. It would make more sense if you ate without me. I'll grab something at the office.'

Ava shoved down an automatic objection as disappointment swamped her.

She was determined not to be selfish. She'd finally realised how successful Flynn was—how many people relied on the success of his property projects. And he'd already taken time off to be with her in Prague.

They'd still have their nights. And if she had time alone she could finalise her lease and move fully into his apartment. Once he'd caught up on the backlog they'd have more time together.

'We'll do it Thursday night, then.' She stroked his leg, circling his inner thigh, revelling in the tightening of muscle beneath her touch.

'You're living dangerously, Mrs Marshall. Unless you want me to ravish you here in the centre of London?'

She leaned closer. 'That sounds tempting, Mr Marshall.' She slid her fingers higher and found her hand imprisoned by his palm.

The car swerved to stop in a no standing zone. Ava turned to warn Flynn, but before she could speak large hands cupped her face and drew her into a kiss that started at hungry and escalated from there.

By the time they broke away, gasping, he'd reduced her to a puddle of lust. The rise and fall of her breasts against her silk gown was sensual torture and her womb clenched hard. She needed Flynn to fill the emptiness.

His hand cupped her breast and her breathing cut off.

'How far to the apartment?' she choked out.

'Too far.'

With a mighty breath he sat back, dragging his hand away. Ava slumped in her seat, desire vibrating through her. She was like a tuning fork responding to his touch.

Flynn peered down the street and she wondered if he'd follow through on the promise in that kiss right where they were. That should have shocked her. A fortnight ago it would have. Instead excitement made her nipples pucker and her mouth dry.

A group of people appeared, talking loudly as they swayed across the pavement. With a soft curse Flynn started the car, pulling into the street.

'I can't go more than a few hours without wanting you.'

He raked his hand through his hair and Ava grinned. She loved the sensual power she was just discovering. He darted a look that burned right to every hidden, feminine place in her body.

'Come to the office and have lunch with me tomorrow.'

'Just lunch? Nothing else?' she teased, delighted at how rough his voice sounded.

Flynn's loving was always wonderful, making her feel like the most adored woman in the world. But there was something entrancing about knowing she got to him on such a visceral level. She looked forward to the day he threw restraint away and loved her with all the pent-up passion she sensed in him.

'What do *you* think?'

Flynn's husky tone grazed the tender skin between her shoulder blades and across her belly, making her shiver again. The car picked up speed, running two lights in succession just before they turned red.

'I'd love to have lunch, but I can't.' Disappointment lodged in her stomach. 'I've got work tomorrow, and I can't take a long lunch on my first day back. There'll be a stack of jobs waiting for me.'

'Tell them you can't make it.' He spun the wheel, turning into their street. 'Better yet, ring and give your notice. Tell them you won't be back.'

'I can't do that!' Her smile died when a street-light illuminated Flynn's features and she realised he wasn't joking.

'Of course you can. Or my PA can do it for you, if you'd prefer.'

Ava sat straighter, a frown pinching. 'You're serious?'

'Of course.' In the gloom she saw him shrug. 'You don't need to work. I can take care of you.'

'I don't want to be taken care of. Not in *that* way.'

He cast her a sidelong glance, eyebrows rising.

Ava stared back. She loved her job. She was good at it. Besides, in working for a charity that supported disadvantaged children, those who'd been neglected or abused, she felt in a small way that she made a difference.

'What made you think I'd want to resign?'

'You want to work in the same office for the rest of your life?'

'No, but...' Ava shook her head.

It was true there wasn't a career path there, but she enjoyed the work and the people and she was learning useful skills. Most important, the steady income gave her the independence she'd prized from the day she'd walked out on her family.

'Do you have ambitions to run the place one day?'

He turned off the street, waiting while the security door of the private garage opened.

'I hadn't thought that far ahead.'

'I'd understand if you had a plan for the future there, but you don't. That job is just a fill-in.'

Ava frowned. 'You make it sound like I was kicking my heels, waiting for you to sweep me off my feet like Prince Charming.'

Flynn's laughter punctured the tiny swell of indignation that bubbled up.

'Prince Charming! No one has ever called me that. I'm more likely to be cast as the Big, Bad Wolf.' Heat simmered in his sidelong look and Ava's insides quivered. 'Maybe that's why I want to eat you all up, Cinderella.'

He spoke slowly, savouring every word, reminding her of the patient, deliberate way he pleasured her when they made love.

'Wrong fairytale, Flynn. That was Little Red Riding Hood.' But there was a breathless catch in her voice. Her mind was already in the bedroom.

The car slid into the basement and he parked neatly near the lift.

'Besides,' he murmured, switching off the ignition and reaching for her, 'what if you get pregnant? Will you keep working then?'

CHAPTER NINE

AVA LAY IN Flynn's arms, her heartbeat racketing, her body humming in the afterglow of climax. He held her close, her head on his chest, his thigh between hers, the musky aroma of sex adding an extra note to the tantalising scent of his skin.

City lights cast a glow into the room. There'd been no time for drawing curtains. No time for anything but falling onto the bed and losing themselves in each other.

The stark intensity of Flynn's expression had told her he was on the edge of control and she'd longed to push him over, walk on the wild side and satisfy his every craving, no matter how demanding. She'd thrilled to the idea of experiencing something as primal as Flynn's unguarded desire. She'd seen flashes of it, but always—even tonight—he pulled back, giving her pleasure, but not the wildness at the heart of him.

She wanted that wildness, that quicksilver energy, that primitive force. She snuggled closer, enjoying the way he hugged her close.

'Is sex always like this?' she whispered. 'So amazing?'

A lazy hand circled her hip. 'With you it is. We were made for each other.'

Ava's breath sucked in. He really did love her as much as she adored him. She was one lucky woman.

'I've been thinking about what you said—about me getting pregnant.'

Flynn's hand paused, then resumed its slow sweep. 'Yes?'

'I'm already on the pill to regulate my cycle, so there's no chance of pregnancy yet.' She paused, sliding her hand over his damp, hair-roughened chest, loving the way taut muscle bunched at her light caress. 'I'm only twenty-four. And we've only just got together. I want to enjoy what we have for a while before thinking about a family.'

'You think children might interrupt our sex-life?'

A little flicker of shock—or was it pleasure?—went through her. Children plural. She was still wrapping her head around the concept of a single pregnancy.

Yet she could visualise Flynn striding across a sun-lit park with a couple of children. A raven-haired little boy, all pluck and adventure, and a girl who adored her daddy, riding on his shoulders.

Ava had never ridden on her father's shoulders. She couldn't remember getting even a hug from him. But

Flynn would be a wonderful father. He came from a loving family. He'd pass that on to their children. He'd always been kind to her and Rupe, never condescending or blaming them for her father's rudeness.

'Do you want children?' It amazed her that she'd never asked. Everything had happened so quickly.

'Yes. But if you want to wait that's okay. The time has to be right for us both.'

Ava exhaled. Things could have got difficult if they'd had opposing views. Thankfully they were attuned, well-matched despite their short courtship. If anyone had told her she'd marry so quickly, and without discussing such important issues, she'd have scoffed. But Flynn had swept into her life and turned it upside down. It should have frightened her, but she was too happy for fear.

'This apartment isn't the place to bring up kids,' he murmured.

'I agree.' Fresh air appealed, but they worked in the City.

'We need to look for a house.'

She smiled. 'With a big garden. Big enough for a dog and a tree house.'

Ava envisaged them having afternoon tea on the grass, or kicking a football with the children. It was such an idyllic picture, and she wondered where it had come from. It wasn't anything *she'd* experienced. But then when she was young she'd escaped reality in the fantasy world of books and her imagination. Maybe it was how she'd envisaged other kids spending time with their family.

'Of course. A rambling house with space for a family. But something with style. A place that makes a statement.'

Ava's brow puckered. Making a statement wasn't what she'd had in mind. But Flynn was in property and he had wealth. He'd want a place he could be proud of.

'I suppose you'll want to entertain a lot?'

'Not all the time. I value privacy. But entertaining will be important, and with you at my side I know it will go well.'

She heard a thread of excitement in his words and felt ridiculously pleased.

'You were wonderful tonight.' His voice caressed her. 'A wife can be an enormous business asset.'

'I know.' Hadn't her mother been just such an asset? She swallowed hard. Flynn's demands would be far more reasonable than her father's. 'I'll help you, Flynn. I'm so proud of you and all you've achieved. You've come a long way. I can only guess at the hard work and determination that got you where you are.'

His hand stopped, his fingers heavy on her hip. 'You're proud of me?'

Ava wriggled onto her stomach, lying over him full-length and lifting her head, propping her chin on her fist. She adored the feel of his body beneath hers.

'Don't sound surprised. Of course I am.'

He didn't smile. 'Some people think I'm ruthless. Tunnel-visioned.'

'They don't know you.' She stroked a finger along the corner of his mouth. 'You'd never do anything bad. Nothing illegal, for instance.'

It took a moment for him to answer. 'No, nothing illegal.'

'Of course not.' She trailed her finger along his hard jaw. 'You're not that sort of man.'

'What sort of man *am* I?' Long fingers twined in her hair, tugging her closer, sliding damp flesh against flesh. Shimmering heat built again in her groin.

'You're hardworking, honest, sexy and incredibly thoughtful. You've got ambition but you know how to laugh.' Ava hitched herself higher, her breasts rubbing his chest. She smiled. 'And you're a fantastic lover, Mr Marshall.'

His eyes held hers for so long she felt the swing and swoop of emotion deep down inside. No one had ever looked at her so intently, taken the trouble to discover the real Ava. Only this wonderful man who'd asked her to share his life. She felt Flynn's gaze probe deep, as if fathoming everything she felt, everything she wanted.

Tenderness was an unfurling bud inside, opening to spread warmth and such heady happiness that her breathing stalled. Ava swallowed, overcome by the depth of her feelings.

Yet Flynn's expression remained serious, the grooves around his mouth digging deep, the line of his brow and the angle of his jaw almost harsh.

Rather than a man in love, he looked like a man in pain.

It must be a trick of the light.

'Cheer up, Flynn. There are worse things than having a wife who adores you.'

She kissed the corner of his mouth, then dusted a just there kiss to the other corner, knowing he was sensitive there. She licked the seam of his lips, shifting so her breasts and belly rubbed him.

Flynn groaned. 'Little witch!'

He clamped her to his stirring shaft and she smiled, a husky, triumphant laugh sneaking from her mouth. She loved the effect she had on him.

With a surge of energy Flynn rolled Ava onto her back. The tumble of their bodies spiked his arousal, testing his limits. Heat ignited as he sank close and fought the need to hammer her, hard and fast.

What had begun as attraction had become an addiction. He needed Ava more and more. Fortunately he had a lifetime to enjoy her enticing sensuality. Being yoked to a wife he didn't desire would have been disastrous.

Her ability to distract him was a surprise. Not just when they were together, but when he worked, enticing his thoughts away from his careful plans.

Ava wriggled her hips and he grabbed her hands, clamping them on the pillow beside her head.

She had no idea what she was inviting. Less than a week ago she'd been a virgin. He owed it to her to go easy, not demand too much, even if she was a fast learner.

Flynn kissed her slowly, deeply, tenderly. His wife was precious and he intended to treat her that way. She was the key, the final piece in his plan to achieve all he'd ever wanted.

Already he had money, power and the grudging respect of his competitors. All he needed was acceptance to secure his place in society, ensuring that he and those he cared for would be secure always.

All his life he'd wanted what Michael Cavendish had. He'd seen Ava's father triumph, ruling his world so nothing touched him or his. They'd led charmed lives, utterly different from his and his parents. Flynn had craved that with a consuming hunger. He'd made it his mission to have all Cavendish had taken for granted. That ambition had driven his phenomenal success.

Ava wriggled again, lifting her hips, and Flynn's thoughts shattered.

He dragged in her sweet essence, shuddering as he held himself in check. He moved carefully, savouring the exquisite sensation of Ava's body clamping around him.

The back of his head threatened to blast off.

All thought of goals and past pain disintegrated as she drew him towards the blazing white light of fulfilment. Her whimper of pleasure, her restless hands on his back and buttocks, the needy rise of her pelvis, tempted him to lose himself.

Flynn fought back, maintaining focus. He was in control always. He had to be.

Slowly he built Ava's pleasure, ignoring the demands of his body for a swift, shattering completion.

It didn't take long. Her soft cries filled the air and soon she was convulsing around him, fingers clutching, her hot gasps hazing his skin.

Finally he let himself go, following her into an orgasm that wrung him dry.

He was left boneless and replete, feeling absurdly as if he'd been washed clean of everything except the imprint of her body.

It was an illusion. It would take more than fantastic sex to cleanse him.

With Ava in his arms he rolled onto his back, gathering her close. The reverberations of their climax still racked his body but that didn't prevent the thoughts surfacing.

For the first time Flynn acknowledged a hint of regret, like a dark smudge on his conscience, marring his satisfaction.

Ava was in love with him. She admired him.

Something sharp jabbed his chest, like a rusty blade scoring deep.

Flynn dragged in a slow breath, telling himself the pain was an illusion.

He was whole and unscathed. He was on track to attain everything he'd ever wanted. Marriage to Ava wasn't just the culmination of his plans, but possibly the best decision he'd ever made. She was the wife he needed. And there were unexpected bonuses. He couldn't get enough of her. Not just her body but her smile, her fresh perspective, that husky gurgle of laughter that always made something like happiness rise in his chest.

He hadn't realised when he'd proposed how much he'd enjoy being married.

Yet it wasn't happiness he felt now. Or even satisfaction. It was disquiet.

She thought him honest.

Until meeting Ava again, he'd prided himself on being just that.

She thought they'd met by chance in Paris.

She'd been caught up in the romance of their meeting, of their trysts in a city designed for lovers.

How would she react if she discovered the truth?

Flynn frowned, dredging up familiar justification.

He hadn't directly lied. He hadn't said anything untruthful. He'd never claimed to have run into her by chance. Every word he'd said to Ava had been strictly accurate.

Which was why he'd never said he loved her.

That rusty blade twisted hard, carving between his ribs and making him catch his breath.

The way she looked at him when she said she loved him… He'd never known anything like it. It made him feel like a triumphant god among lesser mortals. It made him want to be a better man.

It made him wish he could tell her he loved her.

Flynn's arms tightened, hugging her close.

He mightn't be able to do that, but he'd look after her, give her everything she needed. Give her back what she'd once had and lost.

He'd always liked Ava, ever since she was a kid. She'd been the best of the Cavendishes. Even the one time she'd behaved irresponsibly, crashing her car, she'd made him feel protective, not disapproving.

Flynn thrust aside the memory of how much more than protective he'd felt that night. How desire had stirred. How it had coloured his thoughts of her ever since.

He was protecting her now, giving her back the lifestyle she'd been born to. Giving her the chance to mix with the *crème de la crème* of society, enjoying the good things in life. She wouldn't be burdened by long hours of work, like his mother had been. As his wife she'd never have to worry about working.

Most women would be thrilled with a man who could give them that. His lips twisted as he remembered all those who'd unsuccessfully targeted him as a meal ticket.

It was stupid to feel this shadow of guilt. Ava was happy. She positively glowed when she smiled. *He'd* done that—given her the romantic dream she craved and more.

This was no time for doubts.

CHAPTER TEN

'ARE YOU READY?' Flynn's voice came from behind Ava as she stood at the mirror, securing her hair in a classically elegant style that swept the thick waves up and left her neck bare.

She grimaced. It was a pity classical elegance took such effort. She preferred her hair loose. But she'd discovered this last month that Flynn liked her looking glamorous. Wavy hair with a tendency to frizz in damp weather wasn't glamorous.

'Just a minute,' she said through some hairpins.

She shifted in her high heels. After a day in the office, dealing with the bureaucracy surrounding a scheme to build a holiday home for troubled kids, she was exhausted and her muscles were tight with frustration. She'd wanted to put in a few extra hours, determined to sort out the red tape. The outdoor centre for children who'd never had a vacation, and in many cases anyone who genuinely cared, was close to her heart. But Flynn was counting on her. She didn't want to let him down.

Most nights it was the same. They'd go somewhere

exclusively upmarket and mingle with beautiful people. Or, if not beautiful, rich.

Her suggestion that they relax at home hadn't worked so, rather than be completely swamped by Flynn's demanding schedule, Ava had made a point of sticking to at least one night with friends each week. Much as she loved Flynn, she didn't want to lose contact with her friends.

But when did Flynn relax? He spent those evenings she was out working.

Now here they were again, preparing to spend the night networking. She was tired of the chatter of strangers, the game of 'see and be seen'. The need to pretend she was someone who enjoyed these society events. Increasingly, she wished…

'You look gorgeous.' Flynn's deep voice caressed her, sliding across her bare shoulders and neck like a touch.

Ava's tiredness faded. She met his eyes in the mirror.

It was worth it, wearing a long, formal gown instead of one of her bright casual dresses. She did this for *him*.

'So do you.' He was breathtaking. Even with his hair too short for her taste, he filled out a dinner jacket like a movie star. And there was nothing fake about the approval in his eyes as they swept her re-flection in the mirror.

Her nipples peaked in her strapless bra and antici-pation fluttered in her belly.

'Are you sure you want to go out tonight?' She shoved in the last pin and dropped her arms, watch-ing his gaze drift from her face to her throat and breasts. Heat shimmered at the intensity of Flynn's gaze.

He wanted them to be alone as much as she did. It was in his eyes. And in his concentrated passion every night when they returned from some forget-table society function and he took her in his arms.

'Why don't we stay in?' Her voice was husky as she imagined them alone for a whole evening. Not just making love but talking, sharing. 'We never have time alone.'

She missed that. Terribly.

'You've worked the last three weekends, and at night you only have time for a quick change before we go to some function.' Ava planted her hands on her hips, watching with satisfaction as Flynn's gaze flickered to her outthrust breasts. Was it the graze of lace on sensitive skin or the glint in his eyes that made her shiver?

'You'd rather I let my business slide?' His eyes locked with hers and his brow pinched.

'I'd rather you put it in perspective.' She trod carefully. Marriage took adjustment—for them both. She'd made a point of supporting him in his networking because it was important to him. But there were limits. 'You can't go on like this. The hours you put in are unhealthy.'

'The hours I put in are the same as always. Less since we married.' Flynn's big shoulders seemed to bunch, emphasising his latent power. A pulse ticked in his jaw.

Ava cocked her head. 'Are you angry with me?' The thought was so alien it shocked her. Till now there'd been no hint of dissension between them.

Because you agree to everything he suggests.

No. She'd made a conscious decision to support the man she loved. He never asked her to do more than she was comfortable with. Not like her father.

The comparison with her odious father only highlighted how lucky she was. *Flynn cared for her.* Even if he had trouble saying the words, like most men. He was gentle and considerate, generous and passionate.

'Angry?' He shook his head. 'No.'

Yet there was something wrong.

'I worry about you, Flynn. You take on so much and relax so little.' She swung around to face him, her hands gripping the vanity behind her. 'I'm amazed you found time to take a couple of hours off in Paris for that boat ride where we met. And as for a whole week in Prague…' She shook her head. 'Your entire life is work.'

To Ava's surprise colour washed his high cheekbones.

'I'm not accusing you,' she said. After all he'd given her—his love and warmth—she felt she was nagging. Except this wasn't about her, no matter how much she wanted more time alone with him. It was about Flynn.

'I know what I'm doing, Ava.' His tone was as tight as those hunched shoulders. 'Business is booming, but I need to secure it for the future.'

She frowned. His business was as secure as it could get. It was diversified through commercial, residential and tourist developments. Market fluctuations could affect those, but there would always be a core of valuable content as Flynn didn't just buy and sell, but developed and maintained.

'Tonight is important, Ava.'

Slowly she nodded, biting down the retort that every function was *important*. Flynn spent his time deep in discussion with *important* people while she looked picturesque and chatted with hangers-on. Even the businesswomen relegated her to the substratum of 'decorative other'. Ava hated so much about that milieu, but she refused to let it daunt her.

Flynn was so caught up in business he couldn't see that there were better places to be, more worthwhile ways to spend what should be his down time. She needed to help him find perspective, focus on what was important—building their lives together. She couldn't do that by withdrawing from him. It might take time—more than she'd prefer—but eventually she'd help him to find the right balance.

Meanwhile she'd be at his side. Even though she felt unsettled, trapped in a role that made her uneasy.

Was it because it reminded her of her mother's role years ago? To look decorative and enticing, to charm and smile, and not to mind her husband's neglect or his darker machinations.

Ava shivered and rubbed her hands up her bare arms.

'I'm taking Saturday off to be with you.' Flynn spoke and she looked up to find him close, satisfaction in his dark eyes. 'I've found a house. We can see it together.'

'A house?' Excitement rose. *There!* Things were looking up. From his expression, it was something special. 'What's it like?'

'Old, large and rambling. The kitchen and some other rooms need updating, but there's plenty of space. Room for a treehouse and a dog.'

'You remembered.' Ava smiled at him, her hand

on his sleeve. His hand closed over hers, its warmth engulfing her.

'Of course I remembered.'

His smile lifted spirits that had dipped low. Of course he'd remembered. This was Flynn. He might be too wedded to work but she had no doubts about his feelings for her. She was determined to save him from his workaholic tendencies.

'And it meets your needs for entertaining?' A comfortable old house in need of modernising didn't sound the kind of place to entertain VIPs.

'It will meet my needs perfectly.'

His smile broadened and Ava's with it. Once in a place of their own, rather than this soulless apartment, she could make it welcoming and persuade him to stay in more often.

'I'm looking forward to showing you. I think you'll approve.'

'I can't wait.'

The idea of house-hunting together banished her qualms about yet another night on show for Flynn's associates. She felt as if she'd become an attachment to his old life. They needed to move on and build a new life together. It would be fun, viewing places together and eventually finding the perfect home.

'I have something else.' He held out a flat black velvet box. Its embossed gold logo belonged to a famous jewellery house, renowned for designs worn by royalty.

Ava felt a tiny stab of disquiet.

She'd married a wealthy man. He could afford expensive gifts. Yet till now that hadn't included jewellery other than her wedding and engagement rings.

Ava couldn't shift the memory of her father giving her mother jewels to show off her décolletage in the revealing gowns he'd insisted she wore in public. Of the way he'd encouraged other men to admire them and her in ways that had distressed Ava.

'Aren't you going to open it?' Flynn's eyebrows lowered in a crumpled line.

'I'm stunned,' she said, covering her hesitation.

'Only the best for you, Ava.'

He pressed the box into her hand. It lay heavy on her palm.

'Well, open it.'

Hesitantly she did. Blue fire flashed. She felt her eyes bulge, her breath snare.

'Oh, Flynn.' Something worked high in her chest.

'"Oh, Flynn", nice?' he teased.

'How can you even ask?'

'They match your eyes,' he said when she didn't move, just stared.

Tears pricked. As if her eyes could ever be such

a pure, entrancing colour as these exquisite Ceylon sapphires!

'I want to see you wear them.'

His voice was gruff and she jerked her gaze up, catching a tenderness in his expression he usually saved for the bedroom. Her heart turned over. How could she not love a man who looked at her that way?

'Put them on me?' She pushed the box into his hands and turned to the mirror.

The high collar of cerulean blue gems interwoven with diamonds was cool against her skin. It made her pale throat look delicate, almost regal. She felt the platinum chain with its tassel of clustered sapphires and diamonds fall from her nape, tickling the skin between her shoulderblades. She shivered as Flynn traced his finger over its fall, then down to the low back of her dress.

'That's why you asked me to wear this dress?' The low cut was a perfect foil to the stunning jewellery.

He nodded and stroked his hand back up between her shoulderblades. Beneath the ruched silk of the formal gown Ava's breasts swelled and tightened.

'Now the earrings,' he murmured, holding them out.

The sapphire and diamond drops swished against Ava's skin when she moved her head, turning her from passably pretty into full-on glamour girl. The effect was startling—and a little disturbing. But when she turned to Flynn for reassurance she found him watching her with palpable pride and pleasure.

What did it matter if she didn't feel like herself, wearing such finery? That she wasn't used to feeling...bedecked?

Flynn kissed her wrist, his lips hot to her cold flesh.

'You look beautiful, Ava.' He released her hand and stepped back to take her in. 'You'll be the cynosure of all eyes. No other woman will hold a candle to you. You'll be the most glamorous, most richly dressed woman there.'

Ava stiffened. That was what mattered to Flynn? That she was so expensively dressed she was conspicuous?

Something inside stilled, then turned to ice as she saw the triumph in his eyes.

Was her role simply to be visible proof of his immense wealth?

Suddenly the necklace tightened around her throat like a snare.

CHAPTER ELEVEN

BY SATURDAY AVA had put things in perspective. She'd been mistaken about Flynn's motives. The admiration in his eyes at the business gala had told its own tale. He'd stayed at her side all evening, never abandoning her even for business. When they'd made love later he'd made her feel like a princess, pampered and adored.

She shoved aside the thought that she didn't want to be treated like a precious doll. She was just tired. The plans for the children's holiday retreat she'd put so much effort into had completely unravelled due to zoning complications. Ava sighed and rubbed her forehead.

'Problems?' Flynn slanted her a look from the driver's seat.

'A few. The project I'm working on has hit an obstacle.'

'You need to switch off.'

The way he did? But today Flynn hadn't mentioned work. From the moment she'd woken she'd sensed a buzz of excitement in him. She smiled, revelling in the prospect of a whole day with him. Hadn't she told herself things would change? Her patience was finally being rewarded.

'How far from central London *is* this house?' They'd already travelled further than she'd expected.

'Outside London. That's the surprise.'

He darted a grin her way and her insides turned molten.

'Outside? But the commute—'

'It will be worth it. You'll see. This is something special. As for commuting—I'll set up an office in the house and work from there a couple of days a week. It will be a stretch, but I'm sure it can be done.'

'But I'll still need to travel to *my* work.'

Another sideways glance. 'You never know what's around the corner. There may be opportunities for you closer to home. And we'll keep the City apartment for overnight stays. Besides...' He paused. 'Longer term, the country will be better for bringing up children. You said so yourself.'

Slowly Ava nodded. She had said that. Although she'd meant in the much longer term. But they were only looking at the first house. Who knew how long it would be before they found the right place? Besides, the day was bright, the sun shone and they were together.

She relaxed in her seat, alternately watching the

scenery and Flynn's strong, dark features. Some-times she had to pinch herself to believe they were together. The odds against them connecting again in Paris…it didn't bear thinking about…

Lack of sleep must have caught up with Ava. The car passed over a rough patch and she stirred from a doze. Slowly she stretched.

'We're here.'

Flynn's tone jerked her fully awake. There was an excitement in it she'd never heard before from him.

Ava opened her eyes and then blinked, gaping, wondering if she still slept and this was a dream.

The car was following a long gravel drive lined with overhanging trees, their autumn-tinted branches spreading wide. Ahead the road curved, and at the bend stood a grove of massive rhododendrons.

Ava's heart clutched as if an ice-cold hand had reached out and squeezed it.

She recognised the long drive…the rhododendrons.

Eyes wide, she took in the woods to one side, the landscaped park to the other. Her nape tightened, flesh prickling.

Flynn halted the car on an arched stone bridge over a man-made lake.

The bridge had been designed as a perfect vantage point to view the sprawling stone building before them. Ava knew that. Just as she knew the chimneys in the west wing had a tendency to smoke and the butler's pantry was reputedly haunted by the ghost of an old retainer with a fondness for port.

And that even the light from the huge south-facing windows had never been enough to dispel the chill when her father had been in residence.

'Frayne Hall.'

Was that brittle voice hers?

'Surprised?'

Slowly she turned. Flynn's smile was satisfied, full of anticipation. Ava couldn't share it. Her lips felt stiff.

'Stunned.' She swallowed. 'Why are we here?'

Ava hadn't revisited the Hall since the day she'd severed ties with her father and walked out to make her own way in the world.

'I told you we were viewing a house I'd found.'

'*This* house?' Her voice was just a few notes off a screech. Through her bubble of shock Ava saw Flynn frown. She pressed a hand to her chest to still her hammering heart. 'I'd imagined a place in the suburbs.'

Flynn's eyebrows winged up. 'Hardly. I want something special for us.' He shook his head. 'I think you keep forgetting how much I can afford.'

That had been one of the few areas of…not disagreement, but concern between them. Used to supporting herself, Ava was a frugal shopper. But Flynn insisted on the best. 'The best' being designer evening dresses and deliciously sexy shoes far out of her usual budget.

'I thought you'd be excited.' He sounded surprised. 'The place belonged to your mother's family for hundreds of years.'

Six hundred, to be precise. Till the family lost its money and her social-climbing father, with his newly minted wealth and an eye for a bargain, bought it and married the daughter of the house.

A shiver tightened Ava's flesh.

'Come on.' Flynn started the car. 'Let's take a closer look.'

By the time they pulled up at the grand front entrance Ava had herself in hand. Flynn's ideas and hers on a suitable house were obviously wildly different, but they could work on that.

As for Frayne Hall—now the shock was over she *was* curious. Despite the tainted memories, this had been her home for seventeen years. She'd loved much of it—especially when her father hadn't been at home. She'd see the place, satisfy her curiosity, then tell Flynn she'd rather not live here. Simple.

'Ready?'

Flynn was holding her door open before she'd gathered herself. His hand was warm around hers. His smile coaxed and she pushed aside her qualms. The man she adored had organised what he thought was something special for her.

'Ready.'

An hour later they stood in the grand drawing room. The light from the tall windows emphasised the lack of furniture and showed the bare places where paintings had once hung.

Ava preferred it this way: elegant, beautiful and unmarred by the ostentatious displays that had been Michael Cavendish's hallmark. Despite his insistence that his family and home look like something from a glossy magazine, he'd always erred on the showy side. He'd tried too hard to prove he fitted with the wealthy elite he pandered to.

'What do you think?' Flynn rested his arm on the ornate mantelpiece.

'I think you look right at home.'

Ava was used to seeing him in a suit, the epitome of corporate success. She preferred him like this. In jeans and a shirt with the sleeves rolled up he looked relaxed, yet vital and devastatingly gorgeous.

There'd been a light inside him ever since they'd arrived. It reminded her of him years ago. Tousle-haired and vigorous, he'd always seemed more at home roaming the forest or helping his father in the park than inside.

'You should let your hair grow.'

'Sorry?'

Ava smiled. 'I want to run my fingers through your hair.'

'Are you coming on to me, Mrs Marshall?' He snared her wrist, pulling her against him.

'I could be, Mr Marshall.' She read the wicked gleam in his eyes and the last of her reserve fled.

Against expectations, she'd enjoyed revisiting her old home. Whether because she'd temporarily managed to push aside the sour memories of the past or because she was here with Flynn, she didn't know.

'Thank you for bringing me here,' she murmured against his throat as she sank against him. 'It means a lot.'

That had surprised her. For years she'd hated even thinking about Frayne Hall. When she'd seen the painting of it in Flynn's apartment her initial reaction had been horror. But, viewing the place today, she realised her father's posturing and conniving here had been a blink of the eye in the history of the house. Already he'd been relegated to the past, along with the showy pieces he'd bought to impress visitors. The knowledge brought her a sense of closure and, with it, a certain amount of peace.

'It's good to see it again. It's a lovely old place.'

Flynn wrapped his arms around her. 'I knew you'd like it.'

The words riffled her hair and she shut her eyes, enjoying the sensations being with him brought. She inhaled deeply. Was it her imagination or was the woodsy, outdoor tang of his skin more pronounced? She pressed her lips to his collarbone, nuzzling his warm skin.

'I can see a massive Christmas tree just there.' His voice intruded on the beginnings of a sensual fantasy. 'Can't you?'

'Sorry?' Ava blinked as he lifted her chin. Eyes dark as night met hers and the familiar burr of desire hummed in her blood.

He smiled. 'I said I can imagine a Christmas tree there.' He pointed across the room.

To her relief it wasn't where the tree had been erected when she was young. That had been in the vast hall, emphasising the sense of holiday gaiety to all who entered. As if that could make up for the lack of true peace and goodwill on the premises.

'And holly and ivy twining down the stairs.' Flynn pointed towards the open doors and the grand staircase. 'I used to help my father cut the greenery for the house, but I never saw it decorated.'

Of course he hadn't. He'd not been allowed inside

the big house except the kitchen, where his mother worked. None of the outdoor staff had. Her father hadn't cared about his employees—just the people he'd wanted to impress.

'It must have looked wonderful on the night of those winter balls. I remember looking in from the outside, seeing the chandeliers lit on the ground floor and the flambeaux in the garden, leading to the entrance.'

Ava nodded. 'It was certainly spectacular.'

When she was tiny she'd loved the kaleidoscope colours of the guests as they'd mingled and danced. The glitter of light on mirrors and jewels. It was only as she'd grown older that she'd learned to hate the manufactured gaiety, recognising the undercurrents of greed and selfishness.

'We'll make it spectacular again. I can see you greeting our guests. You'll have your hair up and wear your sapphires and everyone will know I'm the luckiest man. We'll open the ballroom again and fill the place.' Flynn strode across the vast room as if measuring it out. 'It's crying out for a big occasion. It was built for that.'

Ava stared, her mind whirling at his words.

'You're serious?'

He couldn't be.

Flynn came back to her, his gaze intense. 'Don't

worry. I'll get my PA on it.' He took her hands, his voice reassuring. 'You won't have to do much more than be your beautiful self and act as hostess.'

Ava curled her fingers around his, clutching hard. 'Just a minute.' She sucked in a shaky breath. 'You're talking as if we'll be *here*. As if we've already decided to buy the place!'

'That's my surprise.'

For the first time she could remember Flynn's slow smile didn't melt her insides. Instead it concentrated her growing chill into an icy lump in the pit of her stomach.

'I've bought it. It's my special gift to you. I knew you'd be thrilled.'

Flynn stared down into clear eyes that outshone the sapphires he'd given her. Today they seemed a deeper blue, dark in contrast with skin that looked too pale.

It struck him that Ava wasn't used to his pace of life. He'd been too caught up in his plans. He should have scheduled more nights at home so she could rest. That job of hers was wearing her out.

He was accustomed to working long hours and fitting in a gruelling round of social functions to further his business interests. Ava wasn't. She looked peaky, with the hint of a tired smudge beneath her eyes. The sooner she stopped working the better.

'I beg your pardon?'

'I've bought it for you. The sale was just finalised.'

Her fingers convulsed around his and he waited for her avid smile. Instead huge eyes met his.

Finally she spoke. 'You *bought* it? But we were going house-hunting *together.*'

Impatience stirred. He'd just presented her with a multi-million-pound country estate and she made it sound as if he'd deprived her of something.

'This is the perfect house for us.' His grip tightened when she would have withdrawn her hand. 'That's why I snapped it up.'

He didn't mention that it hadn't been on the market. He'd made the owner an offer he couldn't refuse because *this* was the house Flynn had been determined to acquire.

'You bought it for me? Because it was my family home?'

She sounded as if she'd had a shock. Flynn supposed she had. Maybe he should have led up to this gradually. Marriage took some adjustment. He was used to making decisions and putting them into action immediately. Perhaps he should have told her of his plans.

'I wanted you to have everything you once had, Ava. This is your family home.' His gesture encompassed not only the Hall but the estate. He laughed.

'Mine too, for what it's worth.' Though he had no sentimental attachment to the damp, crumbling cottage that was the best his parents had been able to provide. 'We're coming home—where we belong.'

He'd never been more certain of anything than the fact that he belonged here, with Ava.

Frayne Hall was the embodiment of everything he'd worked for—the symbol of his success, the jewel in the crown of what had once been Michael Cavendish's empire. Cavendish had ruled like a feudal lord over his family. Now Flynn had built himself an even larger empire. One that supported hundreds of people. One he could be proud of.

Flynn was a man to be reckoned with now—a man shaping the world to his own specifications. A better man than Cavendish, with his bullying ways, had ever been.

'Who says we belong here?' Ava jerked away, to his amazement backing up a step.

'What's wrong? I thought you'd be ecstatic. You said yourself it's a wonderful old place.'

She slashed at the air. 'That doesn't mean I want to *live* here.'

'Big and rambling, you said. Big enough for a family.'

Her laugh was harsh. 'I imagined a cosy house, with room for a couple of children and a dog. Not a mansion that could house all your London office staff and still have room for more.' Ava's shoulders rose and fell with her quick breaths.

'We'll have staff to take care of the place. You won't have to worry about that.' He could easily afford the small army of people required to maintain the Hall.

'It's not the cleaning I'm worried about!'

'Then what is it?'

He stepped closer, but she made no move to take his outstretched hand. Flynn dropped his arm, telling himself she hadn't noticed the gesture. She was caught up in whatever inner turmoil made her lips tighten in an unfamiliar, unhappy line.

Yet an ache started in his belly at her rejection.

It had been years since he'd allowed himself to feel pain. It took several seconds to recognise it.

'You went ahead and bought the place without consulting me.' Her tone was short, her face tight.

'Because it's perfect.' He dragged in a calming breath. He wasn't used to having his decisions questioned. 'You never objected to my surprises before. You loved our wedding, and—'

'That was different.'

The compression of her lips changed to a pout that in other circumstances would have distracted him into kissing her.

'Why?' He paced closer, forcing her to look up.

'It wasn't a decision about our future. It was…' she waved her hand '…short term.'

'I see.'

So Ava was happy for him to take charge of immediate things, but not important decisions about their future. He'd thought she trusted him. Surely marrying him proved that?

He stiffened, annoyance stirring. And something else. Disquiet snaked through him at how she might react if she realised her falling for him had been as much due to his carefully executed plans as her romantic yearnings. His gut clenched.

Nonsense! They were made for each other. In the end it didn't matter how they'd got together. Surely she'd just be happy that he'd made it happen? They were the perfect couple.

'My mistake.' The words sounded foreign on his tongue. 'I apologise.' Not for buying the house, but for not engaging her in the process. That had been his error. 'I should have talked with you and involved you in the decision-making.'

Flynn had been a loner so long he was used to running his own race. He'd shared more of himself with Ava than he had with any woman, but still this was foreign territory. He was learning as he went.

Perhaps the newness of it explained why he wanted

Ava's approval so badly. Why he responded so viscerally to the hint of hurt in her expression.

He wanted her smiling with adoration. He'd grown used to that, enjoying it more than he'd ever believed possible.

It wasn't that he *needed* it, but he wanted it.

With Ava he felt different. Connected. Which was intriguing when he'd never cared about connection before, except with his family. Even his relationships with close colleagues, while genuine, had limits he never crossed, because he was above all focused on success.

It hit him that while he'd changed Ava's life, she'd undeniably changed his. He wanted things he'd never missed before. Like her smiles.

'Oh, Flynn. What am I going to do with you?'

Her mouth turned up in a crooked smile that distracted him from his disturbing thoughts. She shook her head, her lush blonde hair swirling around her shoulders in a way that made him want to forget their argument and find a bed. He couldn't remember being as happy or content as when he had Ava naked beside him.

'You thought you were doing something wonderful, didn't you?'

'I *am* doing something wonderful.' He took her hand, tugging her close.

She laughed—a husky, rueful sound that to his surprise sent relief scudding through him. The churning in his belly eased.

'And so modest!' She sobered. 'I appreciate the gesture, Flynn. It's romantic and generous. But I make my own decisions. Especially on important things. I don't think you realise how important my independence is to me. I don't want anyone, even you, trying to decide for me.'

He read her firm expression and felt again that sinuous, unsettling twist in his gut—only worse this time. As if a venomous serpent writhed there. When she discovered what else he'd done—

No. There was no reason for her to find out.

And if she did she'd understand that he'd acted with her best interests in mind.

That job was draining her...

'This is hardly the place for a quick commute to London.'

Had Ava somehow tuned into his thoughts?

'Even if I stayed in the apartment a couple of nights a week, it's a lot of travelling,' she pointed out.

'We could travel together.'

Surprisingly her eyes shone, as if he'd offered her a treat. She tilted her head. 'I'd like that. Spending more time together.'

So he wasn't alone in craving that. Each week

Flynn found it more difficult to maintain his absolute focus on business. He wanted to take time off and spend it with Ava. Only a lifetime's dedication to building his dream gave him the strength to withstand temptation.

'I could get a chauffeur and a car with a privacy screen.'

'So we could shock the commuters on the motorway?' Ava grinned.

Flynn hauled her against him, enjoying the way she fitted him so exactly. Enjoying even more his relief at her smile.

'So you don't mind that I've bought Frayne Hall?'

'I didn't say that.' Her smile disappeared, leaving her sombre. 'I appreciate the gesture, but even ignoring the fact you didn't involve me in the decision, I'm not sure I want to live here.'

'Why's that?' He'd been convinced she'd be exuberant.

She took a deep breath. 'Living here wasn't much fun, despite how it looked from the outside.'

Flynn frowned, trying to read her expression. 'You're right. It looked wonderful from the outside.'

He'd been jealous of the Cavendishes. Not just of their wealth but of the things it gave them—security, an excellent education, the top-class healthcare that might have saved his father, who'd been on waiting lists so long his illness had progressed too fast to be stopped.

More, they'd had the luxury of free time. They'd enjoyed each other's company whenever they liked. He'd seen them entertaining guests on the lawns or by the lake as he'd laboured beside his father. There'd been days when he'd barely seen his mother, incarcerated in the Hall kitchen—especially when the family was entertaining.

'Appearances are deceptive. It wasn't all happy families.'

A jarring note in Ava's voice caught his attention.

'I know your father could be...difficult with staff...' Flynn spoke carefully, conscious that Ava must have cared for the man. 'But he was devoted to you.' Flynn had seen the arrogant bully soften with his wife and kids.

'You think so?' Ava's expression hardened. 'It was all a lie.'

'Sorry?'

'Your mother didn't tell you?'

'Tell me what?' He didn't like the taut way Ava stood in his arms. He felt a tremor pass through her, and there was a bleakness in her gaze that he didn't recognise.

'My father was...' She swallowed, and to Flynn's amazement he saw her eyes shimmer as if with tears.

'Ava? What is it?' He palmed her cheek, needing to ease the pain he saw.

'I don't want to talk about it.' To his amazement she pulled away. 'Especially here.'

Flynn stared. He felt the ground shift beneath his feet. All his life he'd envied the Cavendishes their easy, privileged lives. Michael Cavendish had been a selfish bastard to his employees, but he'd always seemed an attentive father and husband. The perfect provider and protector.

What had he done to Ava to make her blink back tears? Had the pair fought the last time they'd been together? It must be something like that. He'd been a doting parent. Flynn had seen it time and again. Cavendish had showered his only daughter with extravagant gifts—like a convertible pink Mercedes on her seventeenth birthday.

'All right, we won't talk about him.' He held out his hand. His heartbeat kicked when she put her palm in his. 'Agreed?'

'Agreed.'

'I want you to be happy here.'

She sighed. 'I know you do. I know you bought this as an extravagant romantic gift.'

Romantic? Flynn forbore from explaining that he'd planned to own Frayne Hall from his sixteenth Christmas. He'd sat in a stark hospital room, watching his father die, desperately waiting for his mother to get away from work at the Hall before it was too late to say her goodbyes.

He'd known then that if things had been different—if they'd been rich and powerful—his father wouldn't be there, fading before his eyes, his breath a clattering gasp, tolling out his last hours.

'It's all right, Flynn. I understand.'

Blindly, he tried to focus on Ava's features.

She had no way of understanding.

Maybe that was why he was such a loner. No one else understood his burning drive to turn his life around, to grab control and shape his future. Not even Ava.

'So you're content that I've bought the Hall?' He phrased it as a question, though he knew it had been the right thing to do.

'It's not what I expected or wanted.' She breathed deep. 'I need time to think about it.'

He threaded his fingers through hers. 'It's got huge possibilities.'

Still she didn't look convinced. He suspected it would be harder to persuade Ava to live here than it had been to get her to marry him.

'I can imagine us raising a family here, creating new memories together.'

The spark of surprise in Ava's eyes told him he'd

struck a chord. His confidence rose. So she wasn't completely opposed to the place—just to the memories it harboured.

'Take all the time you need, Mrs Marshall.'

And in the meantime he'd do his damnedest to persuade her.

Flynn bent his head, ploughing his hand through her soft tresses, tilting her head. Cerulean eyes met his. Gently he planted his mouth on hers. For an instant she didn't move, then he swallowed her soft sigh of pleasure. Satisfaction rose. In this, at least, no persuasion was needed.

CHAPTER TWELVE

'I SUPPOSE IN the long run it could be a good thing.' Ava tried to inject a smile into the words, knowing her brother would hear it over the long-distance connection.

'How do you figure that? You *loved* that job. You *must* be hurting.'

Ava's mouth crumpled. Rupert knew her so well. She *had* loved her job, and the sense of contributing to something worthwhile. It had been more than a means of earning a salary.

She stared across the Hall's newly mown lawns to its private forest. When she was little she'd loved to escape there and pretend the world was a happy place. Until her father had discovered her there one day, looking rumpled and grubby, and forbade her access. Maybe she should take herself off to the woods and see if that helped.

'I am hurting.'

She caught a wobble in her voice and dragged in a shallow breath. She hated self-pity.

'The shock made it worse. There was no hint that

things were so bad they'd have to cut staff. The first I knew was when the HR manager called me in for a "chat".'

'Bloody insensitive way to break the news. Especially after all the unpaid hours you put in for them. They're going to regret losing you.'

Ava smiled. Rupe had always been on her side. Not surprising, since it had always been them against the world—or at least against their domineering father.

'I was a small cog in the wheel, to be frank.' She rolled her shoulders and straightened. 'I'm looking for something else. Meantime, there's a lot to do getting Frayne Hall ready to move into. It's a good thing I've got time on my hands.' She paused, hitching a breath. 'Did I tell you Flynn wants to hold a winter ball?'

'You did *not*!' She heard Rupert's shock. 'Are you up for that?' he said eventually, his tone carefully neutral. 'It doesn't sound like your thing.'

Despite the prickle of tension down her backbone, Ava smiled. 'Why don't you just come straight out and say what you think?'

'What? That it's the worst idea I've ever heard? How can Flynn suggest it, knowing what happened that last time?'

Ava paced to the vast windows, watching a van appear in the distance, entering the park.

'Flynn doesn't know.'

'I thought he was there that night. Surely he—?'

'Yes, he was there.' She rubbed her hand up her sleeve to stir warmth into chilled skin. 'But he never knew the full story. Not why I ran away. He wasn't at the Hall itself. He was at his parents' cottage. He assumed I'd been partying and had just taken the car for a midnight spin.'

Her gaze followed the van as it rounded the drive's curve towards the massive rhododendrons where she'd once missed the bend and ploughed her convertible head-on.

She remembered her intense relief when it had been *Flynn* who found her. He'd been gentle, so calm in the face of her distress. The image of him—big, capable and protective—had stayed with her.

Flynn had always been special.

Yet she'd shied from telling him about her father and her life here. Why? Because she was ashamed? Because, although she told herself she hadn't been at fault, she felt *sullied* by what had happened? As if her family's sins marked her.

Of course they did. Why else had she kept herself to herself all these years, till Flynn had swept her caution aside and she'd fallen into his arms?

'Don't you think it's time to enlighten him?'

'He can't change the past. What would it achieve?'

Rupert hesitated. 'I thought husbands and wives were supposed to share?'

'We do. *I* do.' Ava realised her voice had risen. 'The important things.'

'And telling your husband you'd rather be skinned alive than face another winter ball in the old family pile isn't *important*?'

Ava rubbed the gooseflesh that had risen anew on her arm. 'If you must know, I don't like talking about it. It makes me feel sick.'

'I can understand that.'

But Rupert didn't know that even now she wondered if her father had spied something in her—some innate weakness that had made her the perfect tool for his plans.

How deep did the family taint run?

'This ball will be different.' She forced her thoughts to the future, injecting enthusiasm into her voice. 'This will be *our* party. Nothing like the old days.' She paced the length of the window. 'I realised when I came here how I'd shunned the place because of memories. I'm tired of wearing the past around my neck like an albatross. It's time to make new memories. Happy ones—with Flynn.'

It was time to be strong, not to hide from the past.

'Good on you, sis. That takes guts.'

Ava shrugged. Rupert hadn't had it easy here

either—that's why what she had to say was such a big ask.

'It would be much easier if *you* could be here, Rupe.' She paused, hearing his swift intake of breath. 'Would you come for the party? It's been ages since I saw you.'

'I'm not sure if I can get away.'

'Surely you can take a few days off? Please?' She watched the van pull up outside. 'It would give you a chance to get to know Flynn.'

'And lay a few ghosts while I'm at it?'

'That too.' She waited with bated breath.

It was silly—she'd have Flynn by her side for the big party he so wanted. But having Rupert too, when she had to face a who's who of the county and the City's elite, would shore up her resolve.

These months at Flynn's side, stepping back into a world where she had to pretend to be soignée and glamorous, enduring round after round of empty chat with people she didn't particularly care for, had been hard. She kept recalling her father pulling the strings, demanding she look just as he wanted, say and do exactly the right things.

Playing the society hostess in this house, full of memories of her mother's brittle smile, her father's manipulative ways and her own trauma…it would stretch her to the limit. She dreaded it—even though she was convinced it would finally help her face her demons.

Rupert sighed. 'Okay, Ava. I'll be there. For you. Just remember you owe me big-time.'

She smiled, relief hitting her as she sank back against the ancient wood panelling. With Flynn and Rupert here she could do this. She'd prove the past had no hold any more.

Once that was done—once the rush to refurbish the Hall and organise this ball were over—she'd *make* Flynn take time off. They'd build their relationship and make a home together.

'Thanks, Rupe! You don't know what that means to me.'

'Well, if nothing else it will give me a chance to know Flynn. A man who can get you to live at Frayne Hall, even host a ball there, must be special.'

'He is. Just wait and see.'

Yet as she ended the call, absently watching men get out of the van full of the furnishings Flynn had organised, Ava frowned.

Every night Flynn made love to her with a tender intensity that touched her heart and left her more than ever addicted to him. Yet somehow they never managed more time together, even now she was jobless.

Flynn had assured her that once Frayne Hall was ready he'd work from his home office. There would be more time for them once a couple of huge projects were wrapped up. He'd take time off to spend whole days with her, like in Prague.

She understood his need to network. But there had been an unrelenting round of social events.

Ava wanted to let down her hair—literally—and spend quality time with the man she loved. She felt as if she was becoming a cipher, not a real person.

The image of her mother rose. She'd been elegant and charming, but beneath the charm and the tinkle of laughter had been tension, an emptiness that had scared Ava almost as much as the desperation she'd sometimes seen in her eyes.

A clatter drew her attention. They had opened the back doors of the van. Ava slipped the phone into her pocket and headed out, grateful for the distraction.

'Where do you want these?' The foreman gestured to the paintings in the vehicle's cavernous interior.

'It depends what they are. I'll need to have a look.'

Already, with a speed that Ava could scarcely credit, the painters had finished the main ground floor rooms of Frayne Hall and were working upstairs. Flynn had said it was up to her where she placed the items he'd organised, but as she had no idea what he'd bought she'd have to check each piece.

Funny... Usually it was the wife who shopped for

furnishings. Though, given Flynn's schedule, she doubted he'd shopped himself. He'd probably had one of his super-efficient staff do it.

Her brow wrinkled. She should have volunteered. But everything had happened so fast. First the news that Flynn had bought the old place, then her job loss, and then his casual announcement that he had some items being delivered and would she mind being there to supervise?

Well, things would change, Ava decided. If they were going to live here she'd have to take a hand. Especially in their private rooms. Something bright, she decided. Something utterly unlike the pale watered silks, gilt and crystal and child-unfriendly furnishings of her parents' era. Something comfortable and welcoming.

As soon as this delivery was sorted she'd make a list and start some serious shopping.

Following the driver's lead, she stepped up into the van and watched him uncover the first of dozens of paintings, all carefully wrapped and secured.

Familiar eyes met hers. Blue eyes, and the trademark family mouth and chin. Ava stared. The painted face belonged to her great-great-grandmother, refined in pearls and an Edwardian gown.

Ava stared, a sense of *déjà-vu* hitting her. Last time

she'd looked into that face it had been in the portrait gallery upstairs.

The next painting was of a Cavalier on horse-back—another ancestor. Then a study of two boys in satin and lace-edged collars, with a glossy spaniel at their feet.

Her heart pounded as she scanned the stacks of covered canvases. Had Flynn tracked down all the portraits her mother's family had accumulated? How long must that have taken? They'd only been married a couple of months.

She shook her head, bewildered.

'You approve?'

Ava spun around, startled by the familiar deep voice.

'Flynn? What are you doing here? I thought you were in London.' Her heart leapt as he climbed into the van, taking her outstretched hands and tugging her to him.

'I took the afternoon off.'

'You did?' She arched her neck, peering up into his smiling face. Her pulse skittered. Without his jacket and tie he looked like the man who'd wooed her in Europe. The man whose humour and compassion had swept her off her feet.

'I promised, didn't I?'

His voice was a low rumble as he kissed first her

cheek then her mouth, and she sank into him. Dimly she was aware of the driver exiting the van, discreetly leaving them alone.

'One day soon, you said. I didn't think—'

His finger against her lips stopped her. 'I'm here now, with a picnic lunch.'

'A picnic?' Ava's smile became a grin. 'Really?' Had she told him they were one of her favourite treats? One she'd never indulged in till she left home. There was something deliciously decadent about eating outdoors, lying back and watching the clouds pass by. 'Let's go up to the woods. I know the perfect spot. High up on the edge of the forest. It's full of bluebells in spring, but even today it will be lovely, with a fantastic view over the park.'

To think she'd been so discontented just half an hour before. See—Flynn *was* making an effort.

'Whatever you like.'

He kissed her again and her breath snagged. It was almost frightening, the power he had over her emotions. What was it about Flynn that could brighten her day in the blink of an eye?

The answer was easy. He cared for her. Not as a pawn to be played, but for herself. He loved her. He'd showed her in so many ways.

'You're happy about the paintings?' He drew back a fraction.

Ava nodded, turning to survey the canvases. 'It must have taken ages. I can't believe you've found them in the short time since we married.'

His fingers tightened around her waist and it was a few moments before he spoke. 'I have excellent staff. When they know I want something, they make it happen.'

His tone sounded stiff.

'Is everything all right?' Ava regarded him curiously.

'Why wouldn't it be?'

She shrugged. She couldn't read his expression, yet she felt he'd tensed. 'I just wondered.' When he said nothing she spoke again. 'It was a lovely idea.' Just the sort of caring, generous gesture he showed her again and again. 'What else is in here?' She pointed to the other shrouded shapes.

'Furnishings. Pieces for the Hall.'

Curious, she stepped forward. He moved with her, his hand at her waist. Ava loved that Flynn was so demonstrative, always touching her, even when they were at some high-profile event. It reminded her that behind the glitz and glam it was *her* he was interested in.

She lifted some heavy felt wrapping—and froze. In the stillness her breath sawed loudly.

'My father's desk…' Her voice sounded far away.

'It took some tracking down.'

'Why did you bother?'

Ava told herself to drop the heavy material and block out the sight, but her fingers didn't obey. They clutched the fabric like talons.

'It's a beautiful piece. A one-off. I remember admiring it the one and only time I went into the Hall.'

Slowly Ava nodded. It *was* beautiful—massive and imposing, as befitted a man who'd seen himself as ruler of all he surveyed. She'd spent hours studying its intricacies as her father verbally tore her to shreds for various misdemeanours.

One of her earliest memories was of standing, hands clenched, before this desk as he berated her for having the temerity to skip down the hall and nearly collide with some important visitor. Her eyes had been level with the top of the desk and she'd thought if she concentrated hard enough on its carvings she wouldn't cry.

She jerked back convulsively, as if touching a snake, and the heavy felt dropped.

Her eyes darted to the other shapes. What else was Flynn bringing back into the house? She swallowed hard, her throat scratchy.

'Where are you planning on putting it? In the library?'

Despite her father's strictures on her not touching

the books, that had always been her favourite room. Her father had rarely used it, instead turning another room into his study.

'No. I'll use it in my office.'

Ava frowned. 'I thought you preferred a modern style? This is an antique.' She *hated* the idea of Flynn at this desk. It was irreparably stained with her father's imprint. 'Why not get something streamlined—like in your London office?'

'This is in keeping with the ambience of Frayne Hall.'

Ava swallowed a retort that it was exactly that ambience she wanted to change. It was lovely to see the family portraits, but she hadn't missed being watched over by ancestors who couldn't save her from her father's rule. If she had her way there'd be nothing from the past in their home.

'Ava?' His eyes narrowed. 'Is everything okay?'

What could she say? That he'd resurrected her father's ghost by bringing his desk back to the Hall? Surely she wasn't such a wimp that a chunk of carved wood could spoil everything? Flynn had gone to enormous trouble to locate and purchase some of her family heirlooms. Because he loved her.

'Of course everything's okay. So long as you leave me scope to finish the rest of the furnishing. I need to get more involved.' She slipped her hand in his as they moved towards the back of the big van. 'Let's show them where to store this stuff, then we can be on our way.'

'There's one more thing.' The corner of Flynn's mouth curled, grooving a sexy curve into his cheek. 'A surprise.'

His obvious pleasure made her smile, her heart lifting.

'Another one?' Ava surveyed the swathed paintings and furniture. 'You've done enough, Flynn. It's surprise enough that you're here.'

That was what she treasured—time alone with him. Not the material things he could give her. But maybe it wasn't a *thing*. Maybe it was like the picnic—a shared experience.

'Indulge me,' he murmured.

He jumped down, then grabbed her by the waist, swinging her through the air, making her clutch his shoulders. Slowly he lowered her to the gravel, his eyes gleaming in a way that made her heart career wildly.

He leaned close, but instead of kissing her he touched his lips to her ear, making her shiver. 'Ready?'

Ava nodded, her vocal cords too tight for words. It was crazy, but Flynn's tenderness made her that happy.

She'd supported herself since she was seventeen, after walking out of Frayne Hall and never looking back. She was independent, capable, and moderately intelligent. But she'd waited so long for Flynn to share himself with her again—to give her that part of him that seemed so distant in London.

Now he was back—the Flynn she'd fallen in love with.

Ava cupped his jaw, feeling the texture of his skin, the solid bone and the steady pulse beneath her fingertips.

'Ready,' she whispered, and let him gather her to him.

This time he did kiss her, regardless of the removal men, till her head spun and she could swear the autumn sun blazed brighter.

When Flynn pulled back he was breathing hard, his nostrils flared and his chest lifting. His hand in her hair cradled, caressed.

He opened his mouth to speak but a nearby scraping sound reminded him they weren't alone. His mouth twisted ruefully and he turned to give the men directions, telling them they'd be back soon. Then he led her around the side of the house.

'Where are we going?'

'It's a surprise, remember? Close your eyes.'

With Flynn's strong arm around her waist, and his

stride shortened to match hers, Ava had no qualms about shutting them. They walked in silence, gravel crunching. Funny how disorientated she felt. She should be able to tell exactly where they were, but couldn't even tell how far they'd gone.

Finally they halted.

'You can open them.'

She hesitated, enjoying Flynn's embrace and the delicious frisson of anticipation feathering through her.

She opened her eyes—and froze.

Ava's breath stopped. For a heartbeat, then a second, third and fourth, she stood unmoving. Then, like a blow from an unseen axe, sensation hit. Her knees crumpled and she sagged against Flynn.

Her eyes rounded as she took in the car parked in the cavernous garage. In the overhead lighting it gleamed as if it had never left the showroom. On its bonnet was the most enormous bow she'd ever seen—black, to contrast with the powder pink of the chassis.

'It's…I don't believe it.' But even blinking furiously didn't alter what she saw. The latest model Mercedes convertible in pastel pink.

As if someone had taken the car her father had bought her years before and waved a magic wand, updating it and removing the damage done when she'd crashed it.

What had possessed Flynn to give her *this*?

Did she look like a pastel pink sort of woman?

The idea added to her shock.

Was that what she'd become, with her society smile and her formal clothes and the sleek, upswept hair Flynn preferred for their evenings out? How long since she'd worn vibrant colours or her favourite polka dots? How long since she'd spent the evening talking about something important rather than mouthing platitudes?

'Believe it, Ava.' Beside her, Flynn sounded pleased—as if he'd read her shock as delight. 'I remembered the old one and how you loved to drive it.'

Silently, Ava nodded. She *had* loved to drive it. What teenage girl wouldn't? Until her father had made it clear what price he expected her to pay for the privilege. He'd explained with devastating succinctness that everything they had—even the house—rested in the balance as he tried to bring off the coup that would salvage his business. That he needed her co-operation.

Bile rose in her throat. She choked it back, pinning the semblance of a smile on her face. It felt like a rictus grin, but Flynn didn't notice. He was too busy explaining the latest model, its features and gadgets.

Typical man, some functioning part of her brain noted.

But the other part—the feeling, emotional part—felt as if Flynn had ripped her wonderful day apart and tossed her back to the year she was seventeen, when she'd discovered just how vile the world could be.

CHAPTER THIRTEEN

AVA SMILED AND NODDED. Yes, the Hall looked wonderful. Yes, it was good to be 'home', hosting her first party at Frayne Hall. Yes, the ball next month would be a red-letter event.

As if the prospect wasn't like a lump of rock in her belly.

She'd tried to lift her spirits with a dress of vibrant scarlet—a colour she loved. But it hadn't succeeded. She moved among the guests, laughing and feigning interest. No one seemed to realise her smile hid thoughts that were anything but placid.

Plans for the ball and this house party had consumed her. Thinking about them, and the memories they dredged up, made her queasy.

But it was more than that. She felt…dissatisfied.

After months of marriage her dreams of quality time with Flynn were still only dreams. He might work from Frayne Hall sometimes, but that just meant long hours locked in his study. There'd been no more picnics, and precious little time together when they weren't on public view.

Something had to change. There and then she determined to confront Flynn tomorrow. She couldn't go on like this.

He was good at providing material things. But the one thing she really wanted—the man himself—eluded her.

Ava saw him across the throng, talking to a high-profile politician, working the room. He didn't glance her way. How long since he'd held her in his arms except in bed?

She blinked as the throb behind her eyes became a harsh pounding. She longed to escape—pull the pins out of her too tight hair, kick off her high heels and put on her old comfy pyjamas with the cute cow print that always made her smile. Pyjamas she hadn't worn since she'd met Flynn, because he liked her in silk and lace or nothing at all. She'd make hot chocolate, grab an old film and—

'Well, hello, Ava.' The voice froze her thoughts. 'Long time no see.'

She spun to find a florid man with iron-grey hair and a wide smile.

The air ground in her lungs as if she'd breathed in shards of glass instead of oxygen.

Her flute of sparkling water tilted in nerveless fingers, spilling down her dress. Belatedly she clutched it tight, holding it in front of her like a barrier.

She felt her eyes widen, her mouth sag.

'Benedict Brayson.' Her voice was a wisp of sound.

His smile grew, but his eyes were calculating.

A shudder ran down her back, chilling her despite the climate control and the press of people. Hairs stood up on her nape and arms as his gaze trawled her slowly…thoroughly.

'Obviously you weren't expecting to see me, Ava, but I must say I've looked forward to renewing our acquaintance.'

His stare settled on her cleavage and her limbs iced.

'You're even more beautiful now than the last time we met.'

Nausea erupted in her belly and she staggered away—only to come up against someone's back.

Her breathing was shallow and fast. Her pulse accelerated to a frantic roar in her ears. She swung her head, but there was no escape. Every way was blocked by clusters of guests.

He said something but she couldn't hear the words. Mesmerised, she watched those fleshy lips move, the grey eyes glitter avariciously.

She was seventeen again, and horrorstruck, dumbfounded and frozen to the spot.

Then, finally, her brain began to work. With it came a blast of fury so strong she shook with it.

She wasn't going to run. *She'd* done nothing wrong. 'How dare you enter this house?'

His eyes widened. Then he shook his head, his smile returning. 'I have an invitation, dear Ava. From your *husband.* No doubt the estimable Flynn wanted us to renew our acquaintance.'

Flynn flicked his gaze across the crowd, as always seeking Ava. She was his talisman, his lodestone.

He frowned. Even from this distance her pallor was unnatural. She looked as gorgeous as ever. When he'd seen her in that red dress he'd wanted to crowd her back into the bedroom, away from the leers of other men. He'd always liked her in pale, classic colours, but tonight she was vibrant and enticingly sexy. Or she had been. Still stunning, she'd suddenly lost her inner glow.

His brow knitted as he read her stiff stance and the way her face drew too tight, her mouth a hard line.

Murmuring apologies, he ploughed through the crowd, ignoring outstretched hands and invitations to stop.

His eyes were on Ava. She looked…blank…still. And yet with a sense of banked emotion. Concern quickened his step.

'I want you to go.'

Her voice was low, but he caught it clearly amidst

the crowd's noise. He'd never heard anything so frigid. It was hard to believe that voice was hers.

'But, my dear, how *can* I? We haven't had time to get reacquainted.' It was Benedict Brayson—the merchant banker.

Flynn stopped beside Ava, sliding his arm around her waist. She vibrated with tension.

'There you are, darling.' He looked into her set face but she didn't shift her eyes from Brayson. It was as if she were mesmerised.

Brayson broke the silence. 'Ava and I were just—'

'Get out of here. *Now.*' She almost spat the words at Brayson, her venom shocking Flynn. 'I don't want you near me.'

'But your husband *invited* me.' The older man patted his breast pocket as if to confirm it. Flynn read avid excitement in his eyes. 'Didn't you, Flynn?'

Brayson's enjoyment of the situation goaded Flynn's temper. It didn't help that the man reminded him of every pompous, arrogant ass who'd ever lorded it over him or his family.

Flynn slipped his arm from Ava and surged forward into Brayson's space. He didn't know what was going on. He'd sort out the details later. Whatever it was, he knew Ava wouldn't act like this without reason.

'It's time you left, Brayson.' His jaw was so tight the words came out as a growl.

The other man goggled, but stood his ground, his smile placatory. 'Now, now, my dear chap. It was just a misunderstanding. The little lady overreacted, but I forgive her.' Flynn heard Ava's hiss of indrawn breath. 'You wanted to consult with me about—'

Flynn's fingers closed around Brayson's collar, twisting, drawing the man up to his level. Dimly he heard the chatter around them stall.

He leaned in. 'Either go under your own steam or I'll eject you myself.'

Watery eyes bulged. Brayson's face turned puce and he spluttered like a fish out of water. 'I'll go,' he croaked.

Even then Flynn would have marched him out if it hadn't been for Ava's hand clutching his sleeve.

'Let him go. You've got guests.' She tugged hard. 'Flynn. Please.'

Reluctantly he released his grip, watching Brayson slump back on his heels, his hand going to his wattled throat. An instant later he lurched through the crowd towards the door. Heads swung, following his progress, then turned back to Flynn and Ava.

He wanted to clear the room. Tell them the party was over. Take Ava somewhere private.

He turned, looking down into glowing blue eyes. 'Are you all right?'

'I will be.' Her voice sounded odd.

'Come on. I'll get you out of here.'

She tilted her chin. 'No. This is our party—our house. I'm not running away.' She pulled back in his hold, glancing around at the guests watching so eagerly. 'Come on, Flynn. It's over. We have a party to host.'

'What was that about with Brayson?'

Flynn tore off his bowtie as he strode across the room, eyes fixed on Ava. The stragglers had left and at last they had privacy.

She sat on the side of the bed, unbuckling her shoes. The gentle curve of her body and the slender vulnerability of her neck evoked a balling tension in his gut. She looked fragile. So pale still that her skin seemed translucent.

Yet when she looked up her eyes were brighter than he'd ever seen them. There was a palpable energy about her.

'Thank you for that.' Her voice was husky, but strong.

Something punched him in the solar plexus, sucking the air from his lungs. The force of her smile.

It wasn't a smile of joy. It was too tight, too fierce.

She looked as he'd never seen her—stronger and yet conversely more *exposed* than he could remember.

'Thanks for what? Not making the scene worse by chucking him out bodily?'

His hands clenched. He'd wanted to wrap his fingers around Brayson's pudgy neck for that sly, salivating look he'd given Ava. No man treated Flynn's woman that way.

She dragged the pins from her hair and sighed, rolling her shoulders as her gold hair fell in thick waves around her shoulders.

Flynn watched it curl around her fair skin, glinting. He admired her beauty when she was dressed to the nines, hair up and make-up perfect. That was the way he'd thought he preferred her, as the polished hostess.

Yet there was another sort of perfection, he'd come to realise. An intriguing beauty in the rumpled, unguarded woman who gazed intently into his eyes when they made love. In her dishevelled pleasure when he kissed her till her lips were plump and pouting and her eyes shone. In the cute, secretive smile she wore when she tried to seduce him from his work. In her laugh, full-throated and husky. It was animation that made Ava truly gorgeous. Her happiness, her enthusiasm.

He hated seeing her distressed.

'Thank you for standing up for me. For taking my side.'

Flynn frowned. 'Of course I took your side. You're my *wife*.'

To his astonishment Ava blinked and looked away, putting the hairpins on her bedside table, but not before he saw the over-bright glitter of her eyes and her convulsive swallow.

'Ava? What is it?'

Instantly he was beside her, hip to hip on the bed, his arm around her waist. She felt warm and right in his hold.

She lifted her shoulders jerkily, head averted. 'It means a lot that you confronted him. I know tonight was important to you—our first party at the Hall.'

Flynn's brow pinched as he viewed her taut profile. 'You thought because of that I'd let him insult you?' There'd been no mistaking Brayson's air of superiority, or his bullying.

Ava busied herself removing her earrings.

'Ava, talk to me.' He took her chin and gently turned her face.

Her dark lashes were spiked, her eyes shining with unshed tears. She bit the corner of her mouth and something inside him turned over as he saw it tremble.

Ava gave a crooked smile that carved his innards. 'I'm not used to anyone standing up for me.'

The admission filled the room with unspoken questions. He saw in her eyes, heard in her voice that this wasn't some throwaway comment. This *mattered*.

Whatever the issue, it ran deeper than that ugly scene tonight.

He thought back to what he knew of her past. Michael Cavendish had always got his own way, bullying staff and strangers to do so. Flynn had seen how the other man's family benefited as a result. Their lives had seemed easy. Now he wondered...

Or perhaps it was nothing to do with her father. Maybe she'd crossed paths with Brayson in London?

'Tell me.'

'He's a detestable man and I couldn't bear to have him here. I didn't know you'd invited him.'

'He's heavily involved in a project I was considering.' His arm tightened around her waist. 'I won't do it now.'

'Just like that?' Her eyes widened.

'Just like that.' He swiped his thumb over her bottom lip, then pressed a kiss there. Her sweetness tempted him but he dragged himself back. 'Now, tell me what's going on.'

'I haven't seen him in years.' Her eyes shifted from his. 'He took me by surprise, that's all.'

'That doesn't explain anything. *Tell* me, Ava.'

Flynn watched her pull in a deep breath, her breasts rising beneath the rich, gleaming red of her dress, and his chest squeezed. He needed to look after her. She was his now. Hadn't his whole focus been on building himself up to protect what was his? His mother, himself, and now Ava?

'How can I help if I don't know the problem?'

'I...' She bit her lip, hands twisting in her lap.

'Yes?'

'I met him that last year—at the Hall. He was a guest, staying for the ball.' Her voice was small. 'He was an associate of my father.' She gave a huff of laughter and suddenly she didn't sound weak at all. 'I didn't like a lot of the people he brought home. For the most part they were self-centred and unscrupulous.'

'You meet all sorts in business. You don't have to *like* the people you associate with.'

She shot him a sideways glance that was all azure fire. 'Don't you?' She looked away. 'My father seemed to attract the horrible, slimy ones. Maybe because they were so like him.'

Flynn stared. He'd known from what she'd told him—more from what she'd avoided telling him— that there'd been some problem between her and her father. But he hadn't imagined the antipathy ran so deep.

It was one thing for *him* to know Michael Cavendish's faults. Quite another for his beloved, favoured daughter to call him horrible and slimy. Ava's comprehensive dismissal of the man shocked him. Flynn couldn't remember her saying a bad word about anyone until tonight. Unlike him, she had a sunny disposition, open and generous.

Flynn waited. He stroked her bare arm, reminding her she wasn't alone. 'Whatever it is, it's festering inside you, Ava. Wouldn't it be better to share?'

Again that sideways stare. This time longer, her scrutiny so intense he felt it sear him.

Her lips twitched. 'Says the man who never talks about his feelings.'

Flynn tugged her closer, relief shooting through him at that glint of humour. 'I'm a guy. It comes with the territory.'

Besides, feelings weren't his forte. Focus and determination were.

Her gaze slid to the far side of the bedroom. 'My father was a selfish, cruel, heartless man. He never cared for us except as extensions of himself. He didn't see us as people but as tools to be manipulated to get what he wanted.' Her mouth compressed. 'He was obsessed with prestige and power. With shaking off his working class roots and being someone *important*.'

That tallied with Flynn's assessment. He'd admired the way Michael Cavendish had pulled himself from nothing to create an empire where he and his family were untouchable, safe and secure. What he hadn't guessed was that he'd been just as ruthless with his own family.

'All our lives Rupert and I were controlled, judged and punished—not because what we did was right or wrong, but on whether it suited the image our father wanted to present to the world. We had to be polite and socially adept. Our manners had to be polished at all times.'

The words spilled faster, her breathing growing choppy.

'We weren't allowed to be kids. We were too busy learning to be perfect—at least on the surface. I learned to ride and play tennis not because I wanted to but because that was what rich kids did. I had to win gymkhana events and anything else I tried. Every activity, every friend, was carefully vetted and approved. I could only mix with the *right* people.'

She shook her head.

'You wouldn't believe the pressure on poor Rupe to excel at sports and at school, or the thrashings he got if his results weren't up to scratch. And when he developed a stutter!' She shuddered.

Fire blazed through Flynn's lungs. 'Your father beat you too?'

'No. He had other ways.' She paused long enough for the hair to stand up on the back of Flynn's neck. 'It wouldn't have done for me to sport bruises. I was his showpiece—the dainty, *perfect* daughter.'

She bit out the words with a sourness that revealed hidden depths of pain.

'I had to look not just pretty, but elegant and self-assured. I had to charm everyone I met—just like my mother.' Suddenly she stopped, swallowing hard. A shudder racked her.

'Your mother?' he prompted softly.

Ava sat silent for so long he thought she wouldn't say any more.

'You know, I always envied you your mother.' She turned in his hold and he saw her painful half smile. 'I barely remember your father, but your mum was always comfortable to be around. Caring and warm. I spent hours daydreaming about being part of a family like yours.'

Now, *that* surprised Flynn. He'd never thought of anyone envying him his childhood. He'd taken the love his family shared for granted, focusing instead on what they *didn't* have.

'That's one of the reasons, even as a girl, I knew you were decent and trustworthy. Knowing your mother, how could you be anything else?' Ava sat straighter. 'Like the night you rescued me when I crashed my car. I knew I was safe with you. You were always good to me.'

Flynn met her gaze and felt something crack inside. He took a slow breath, telling himself that the strange, gutted feeling was nothing. Yet it wasn't. It was something to do with the way Ava looked at him. With such trust and love.

He swallowed hard, shoving aside his long-dormant conscience. It had stirred too late. All that mattered was that he was here to look after her. The ways and means he'd used to get here didn't matter.

'Your mother was cold?'

'Not cold. Distant. Afraid of *him*, I think. I don't remember her ever intervening or taking our side. He didn't marry her for love, but for her social position and pedigree.' She paused, nostrils flaring as she looked at some distant point. 'I'm not sure what she was like in her youth, but she became the perfect Stepford Wife. She did anything he wanted. *Anything.*'

She paused, her breath loud in the silence.

'He used to use her as…' She shook her head. 'I

don't know. Bait. Or as a reward.' Ava's hands came up, rubbing her arms as if to dispel a chill.

'What do you mean, a reward? For whom?'

Shadowed eyes locked with his. He read pain so profound it created an ache in his belly.

'For other men. Men he was doing business with or wanted to.'

Flynn opened his mouth but couldn't think of a thing to say. He stared, willing Ava to say she didn't mean what he thought she did. Instead she regarded him steadily.

He'd known Cavendish was ruthless, but he'd never imagined him sharing his wife with other men to grease the wheels of commerce. The idea was utterly repugnant.

'She was beautiful, you know.'

'I know. I remember.'

To his youthful eyes Mrs Cavendish had been a stunning beauty—slender and gorgeously dressed, always perfect, like an old-fashioned movie siren. She'd never had to slave long hours in a kitchen, struggling to support a son and an ailing husband.

'He used her—made her into a *thing*, not a person. A prize to be won.' Bitterness laced Ava's words. 'It was all very discreet, but every year we had guests staying for the week of the winter ball. And I'd see things…' Abruptly Ava looked away.

'He did the same with me.'

The words were so shocking it took far too long for their meaning to sink in. When they did everything in Flynn froze. Even his heart stalled and the breath splintered in his lungs. His hand on her shoulder went nerveless.

'I don't understand...' he said when he could finally muster his voice. How could Michael Cavendish have used her that way? His skin crawled. 'What sort of man could *do* that?'

She was his *daughter*!

Besides, she'd still been a virgin when they'd married.

'Ava. Look at me.'

Her head swung around and the sheer devastation in her eyes blanched his soul. Then her eyelashes fell, hiding her gaze. But the high spots of colour on her otherwise pale face told their own story.

Flynn felt ill. Because of the murky past she'd revealed, but also because for the first time she was hiding from him.

In one urgent movement he scooped her up and swung her close, sitting her sideways across his lap, her legs draped over his thigh. He tucked her head beneath his chin and cradled her close, rocking her.

She burrowed in and an emotion he couldn't name swamped him.

'I'm glad I've got you, Flynn. I love you so much.'

That ache started again, high in his chest. If he didn't know better he'd think it was his heart. It had to be something far more prosaic. He'd forgotten to breathe, that was all. He'd been so caught up in her revelations.

A long time later, she spoke.

'It started the same as every winter ball, only that was the year after our mother died. So I had to be the hostess.' She shifted uneasily on his lap.

Flynn held her gently, stunned that she'd kept all this to herself.

'The house was full of people our father wanted to impress. People with money or influence. With business opportunities he wanted to exploit. I found out later he'd been in financial trouble for some time, but you'd never have known it. He was always a lavish spender on things outsiders would notice.'

He watched her pleat the fabric of her skirt.

'He'd bought me a new wardrobe—evening gowns, especially. He said I needed to look the part if I was going to be half the hostess my mother had been. I didn't get to choose the clothes or I'd have picked something bright and modern. They were just delivered one day…lots of chic, glamorous gowns.'

She shook her head, an unhappy laugh escaping.

'I'd never worn anything so low-cut. They made

me uncomfortable. Plus the gowns were all white. Every single one of them.'

Flynn remembered that night. She'd worn a full-length dress that shone like spun pearls in the moonlight. Her bare shoulders had been scratched and her cleavage might have distracted him in other circumstances. A slash of scarlet lipstick had smeared across her cheek. She hadn't looked at all like the little girl he'd remembered from his youth.

'What's wrong with white?' Flynn frowned, realising he'd missed something.

'Nothing. Except he'd done it for a reason. Why do you think brides wear white?'

'Tradition?'

As he said it he recalled Ava's insistence that she wouldn't wear it the day they married.

'It's a symbol of virginity.'

In the silence he heard her swallow. Her hands clenched her dress tighter.

'I didn't realise at first, but he was showing me off to his guests. Not all of them, but a select few who knew what he was doing. Apparently I was the prize.'

'Tell me it's not what I think.' Flynn didn't recognise his own voice. This was a nightmare.

'I wish I could.'

Abruptly she moved, leaning back in his arms, her

gaze colliding with his. Her face looked pinched and pale but her eyes blazed.

'He was desperate for money and sponsors for a new project he thought would save him. There were three men he was courting—all of them staying in the house.'

She paused as if gathering her strength, her mouth drawn down in pain.

'He was…auctioning me off. My virginity was apparently a drawcard.'

Flynn heard the words but could barely believe them.

'I was to go to the highest bidder—the one who gave my father what he needed. Brayson was one of them.' Her mouth twisted and her pain transfixed him as surely as a knife thrust through his belly.

Flynn fought for air. It had grown too thick for him to inhale. Fury boiled in his veins. 'And I let the bastard walk out of here tonight. If I'd known—'

'Flynn! That hurts.'

'Sorry.' He forced his arms to loosen so she could breathe, sliding his hands in what he hoped was a soothing stroke.

Sitting still was the hardest thing he'd done in his life. His body hardened, every nerve quickening for battle. Raw hatred filled him—for Cavendish, for the other men who'd played his despicable games, even for her mother, who'd left her at such a man's mercy. He needed an outlet for the fury filling him but it would have to wait. Ava needed him.

'What happened?'

'The night of the ball one of them sent me a box of long-stemmed red roses.' She swallowed but kept going. 'It was a sign that the auction was over. That he'd…won me.'

'Brayson?' Flynn would rip him apart.

'No, someone else. He died a couple of years ago.' No mistaking the shuddering relief in her voice. 'But Brayson knew. He was there that night, watching me all through the ball. Knowing that at the end of it I was expected to—' her voice cracked '—to go with the winner.'

She sighed. 'It went on for a lifetime. Hour after hour of being gawked at, drooled over, until I couldn't stand it any more. My nerve broke and I started guzzling champagne to give me courage.'

'That's why you were drunk at the wheel.' He'd been surprised at the time, he recalled. It hadn't seemed in character.

She nodded. 'I couldn't go through with it. I wasn't taking the car for a joyride that night. I was escaping. Not that I got far.'

'You should have told me. I would have looked after you.' Flynn cursed his obtuseness. Why hadn't he probed further? Why hadn't he questioned her behaviour?

Ava's hand on his chest stopped him. 'You *did* look after me. I can't tell you what that meant. But I had to return the next morning. It was stupid to run off that way. I had to face my father one last time and tell him I was finished with him.'

She huffed out a tiny laugh that held a thread of steel as well as distress.

'Besides, I'd raced out with nothing—not even a jacket. There were things I needed.'

Flynn tried to imagine her confronting the father who'd tried to sell her in a sordid business deal, but his imagination failed. It must have taken courage. More courage than he'd ever imagined Ava would need.

'Your brother didn't help you?'

'Rupe was at school in disgrace, after flunking too many subjects. Our father didn't want to see him.'

'So you had no one.'

Flynn's thoughts kept circling back to the memory of Ava that night—so beautiful, but so distressed. He'd assumed that when she returned to the Hall, whole and sober, all would be well. It lacerated him to realise she'd been utterly alone.

'Why didn't you tell me? I would have helped.'

Her eyes locked with his and something tumbled

over inside him, as if internal organs were rearranging themselves.

'I know you would have.'

She leaned nearer and he breathed in the scent of her skin—roses and sweet woman.

'But if my father had found out it would have meant dismissal for your mother. I couldn't do that to her.'

Flynn covered her hand with his. 'I wish I'd known.'

He didn't tell her his mother had already agreed, at his urging, to leave. The tragic irony of Ava trying to protect his family struck him.

'There's nothing you could have done. I did what I needed to by leaving. I never saw him again after I told him what I thought of him,' she said.

How hard had that been? To leave a life of luxury and fend for herself at seventeen, with no family and, he suspected, no money? He doubted she'd had the street-smarts of a lot of teens, given her upbringing.

That had taken backbone.

Pain was still stamped on her features.

'There's more, isn't there?'

'Not really. Just...' She drew a breath, her gaze shifting. 'I've always wondered if my father saw something in me—something...I don't know...*promiscuous*. Something that made him think I'd be right for—'

'Stop right there.' Flynn battled to keep his voice steady. How *could* she think like that? He cupped her chin, drawing her face up so he could look her in the eye. 'You're not to blame for your corrupt father. You were a kid. And, far from being promiscuous, you were a virgin when we married.'

'Only because the whole experience put me off men.'

'Until you found the right one.' He stroked her cheek with his thumb, tenderness welling. 'You had a traumatic experience, but what your father did was down to him. It had nothing to do with you.'

Flynn willed her to believe him. He couldn't stand her thinking any of it was her fault.

'And instead of going off the rails you fought back. You stood up for yourself and built a whole new life rather than let him brutalise you.' He swallowed hard, appalled at what she'd faced. 'I'm proud of you, Ava.'

Her slow smile made his heart stutter. It was like watching the sun break free of clouds.

'I'll make sure you never have to deal with Brayson again.' It would give Flynn great satisfaction to deal with him personally. 'And the other one. Tell me his name.'

Ava tilted her head, regarding him steadily. Did she read in his expression the surge of violent heat?

The need to wreak vengeance on the men who'd done this to her?

'There's no need. It's over.'

Flynn breathed deep. It wouldn't be over till he'd dealt with them.

'Really, Flynn.' She leaned closer, her expression intense. 'You've already made it better.'

'Hardly.' Ejecting Brayson from the Hall didn't go anywhere near seeing that he got his just desserts.

Ava shook her head. 'You don't understand. When you took my part, without even asking for an explanation…'

She blinked, and to his horror her eyes filled.

'Ava, don't.' He brushed his thumb under her eye, stopping the overflow.

'It's okay.' Her smile was unsteady, but real. 'Truly. For years I've felt I carried this…this taint. I tried shoving the past into a dark hole and pretending it never happened. Tonight it came out into the open, and you know what? I'm glad.'

She dragged in a deep breath.

'It showed me I'm stronger than I thought. And it brought home how wonderful it is to have a man who loves me like you do—who trusts and supports me and stands up for me. I'm so used to standing up for myself, I can't tell you what it means to have someone fighting in my corner.'

Her eyes shone like a glimpse of heaven.

'I couldn't ask for a more loving husband.' She pressed soft lips to his and he felt himself melt. Or was that his conscience?

How could he, of all men, live up to her impossibly high expectations? It shocked him to realise how much he wanted to.

CHAPTER FOURTEEN

'YOU'RE SURE THIS is the place?' Flynn peered through the windscreen wipers at the wind-lashed pavement. Despite the lunch hour, it was almost deserted as people avoided the weather.

'I'm sure.' Ava smiled. 'You're not the only one to know London. I've lived here for years too.'

This was her territory, just streets from where she'd once worked.

'I'll see you inside the restaurant.' He switched off the ignition.

'No, you won't.' Ava put a hand on his arm. 'Really, Flynn. There's no point you getting soaked too.'

He'd been so protective since the night she'd told him about Benedict Brayson and her father. She'd watched shock etch his face, his olive skin turning close to white.

Flynn, like everyone else, had only seen what her father had wanted them to: the perfect Cavendish family. The ugly truth had stunned him.

'I'll stay with you till your friend arrives.'

'You're due at a meeting in fifteen minutes.'

The meeting was supposedly the reason he'd driven to London, though Ava wondered if Flynn had invented the excuse rather than let her travel to the city alone. She shook her head, torn between exasperation and pleasure at his attentiveness.

This past fortnight she'd felt closer to Flynn than she had since Prague. He'd cut back on social engagements, he finished work at a reasonable time and they'd spent the weekend together.

On Sunday they'd tramped the estate, reviewing the refurbishment of the estate cottages—a particular priority with him. They'd shared a flask of coffee and spiced gingerbread at her favourite vantage point on the high ground near the woods, surveying the estate. And they'd ended the day in their big spa bath, sipping champagne, till the wine had been forgotten in the exquisite pleasure of Flynn's loving.

A smile tugged Ava's lips. At last her workaholic husband was realising there were more important things than commerce.

If she'd known her revelations would have such an effect she'd have shared them with him long ago.

'What are you smiling at?' He cupped her face.

Her heart flipped at his expression. Her smile softened into a pout as he rubbed his thumb over her bottom lip, reminding her of how he'd kissed her when they'd got into the car at Frayne Hall. His lips had lingered, tasting, sipping, as if he couldn't get enough, yet his eyes had gleamed not with desire but with tenderness.

Flynn might never say out loud that he loved her. But he proved it in other ways. With his body, his care and thoughtfulness.

'I'm such a lucky woman.' She leaned in, planting a kiss square on his lips.

Instantly he responded, drawing her close.

Finally she put her hands between them. 'The car's fogging up.'

One dark eyebrow rose rakishly. 'You don't really want lunch, do you?' His eyes danced with ebony fire.

Ava's body grew tight, her nipples pebbling and the low buzz of desire humming in her blood. She had to force herself to sit back.

'You have a meeting, remember? And I—' she darted a look at her watch '—don't want to be late. I'll see you later.' She reached for the door.

'I'll collect you.'

Ava shook her head. 'Sarah and I are shopping afterwards. I'll meet you at the apartment.'

'You'd rather shop than be with me?' Flynn looked so taken aback she laughed.

'Wait till you see what I buy.' She waggled her eyebrows suggestively. 'I think you'll enjoy it.'

'In that case, you have my permission to shop all afternoon.' His hand grabbed her as she opened the door. 'But be back by six. I have plans for this evening.'

Somewhere between her mouth and her chest her breath disintegrated, leaving her bereft of oxygen. The slumberous promise in Flynn's eyes did that.

Tugging her hand free, she blew him a kiss and forced herself out into the gusty rain. She'd rather spend the afternoon making love with Flynn. But it had been too long since she'd seen her friend.

In a few hurried steps she was inside the restaurant, watching the Aston Martin pull into the traffic.

'Ava! Over here.'

Sarah, her friend and one-time manager, waved from a booth. Ava smiled and threaded her way through the tables. She took off her jacket and slid into the seat opposite, beaming.

'It's so good to see you, Sarah. I'd hoped to catch up with you before I left.'

Sarah had been away at the time, and that had made the news of Ava's retrenchment even harder to bear.

'I've missed you too.' Sarah put her elbows on the table, leaning forward. 'I couldn't believe it when I heard you'd resigned. You must be absolutely smitten with this man of yours.' She grinned. 'But marriage agrees with you. You look fabulous.'

Ava stilled in the act of looping her shoulder bag over the chair. 'Who said I'd resigned?'

'What do you mean? Everyone knows. We've had a hard time trying to replace you. You had such passion for the work.' She shrugged. 'But I understand you wanting time with your husband. I hear he's gorgeous. And as for starting a family...' Her eyes dropped to Ava's waist.

Ava stiffened. 'We're not. Starting a family.'

'You're not?' Colour etched Sarah's cheeks. 'I'm so sorry. I thought...' She shook her head. 'Sometimes these things aren't straightforward.'

'No, I mean we don't have plans for children yet. Maybe in a couple of years.' She paused, seeing Sarah's confusion. 'Who told you I'd resigned?'

'The CEO. He said he took the call.'

Ava sank back, her brain buzzing. 'He took the call? But I didn't call him!'

The first she'd known was being told by the HR manager that her job no longer existed.

'Ah, that explains the confusion. He said he spoke to your husband.' Sarah paused, her eyes widening. 'He did ask me not to talk about it with the others, but I knew with you it wouldn't matter.' She leaned close. 'I was sorry you decided to go. We made a good team. But on the plus side that huge donation your husband made when you left was a godsend.'

A chill prickled its way, vertebra by vertebra, down Ava's spine. She swung her gaze around the restaurant, half expecting evidence that this was a dream, or a hoax set up for a reality TV show. But the room remained the same.

She spread her hands flat on the table and forced out the words that for some reason she didn't want to speak. 'What donation?'

Sarah snorted. 'Oh, to have so much money you lose track!'

'I'm serious, Sarah. What donation?'

Her friend stared, her smile dying as she finally seemed to register Ava's expression.

Did she look as sick as she felt? Ava told herself it was a misunderstanding. But one thing she knew: Sarah was sharp as a tack. If there was a misunderstanding, it wasn't hers.

'The multi-million-pound donation your husband made personally and on the quiet. The CEO was impressed that he insisted on being a totally anonymous donor.'

Ava clutched the table, as if that would stop the room tilting. She hardly dared breathe. She felt one sudden move might shatter her and her sixth sense warned of impending disaster.

'Are you sure?' Her voice wasn't her own, but then neither was her body. She felt curiously distanced from the conversation—as if she watched it from afar.

Sarah nodded, frowning. 'He said it was his way of making up for the fact you wouldn't be working with us. Obviously he values you highly.'

'Values you highly.'

Ava quashed the bitter laugh as she rammed the last of her clothes—her *old* clothes, not the ones Flynn had bought her—into a suitcase. The one she'd brought with her when they married.

A shudder ripped through her at the memory of Flynn carrying her over the threshold here in the London apartment. She the blushing bride and he…

She rammed the case shut and flicked the lock, hauling it off the bed and out to the foyer. The battered case looked out of place against the expensive furnishings.

She didn't belong here.

Desolation waited to devour her, if she let it. Already it gnawed at her insides.

Anger was by far the easier option.

She stalked back to the bedroom. What else did she need? Most of her things were at Frayne Hall, but she couldn't go back there.

Bile rose and Ava gagged, grabbing the door-jamb for support. It wasn't just Sarah's news about Flynn's dealings with the charity where she'd worked. That had been only the start. After Sarah's bombshell Ava had done some digging and had been sickened at what she'd discovered.

It was amazing what some well-placed phone calls achieved.

If only she'd made them months ago!

Flynn hadn't hidden his tracks well. Why should he? He knew she was besotted, always accepting what he did at face value. Always making excuses for his managing ways.

What a fool!

Setting her jaw, Ava snatched up her coat and bag, trying to ignore the pain threatening to consume her.

There was nothing else of hers here. The bedroom looked as barren as the day she'd arrived.

As barren as her aching heart.

As barren as Flynn's black, conniving soul.

She spun on her heel, forcing herself to concentrate on what came next: a taxi, a room for the night—anything but facing the disaster her life had become.

'Ava?' A tall figure filled the doorway. 'What's that suitcase in the foyer?'

She slammed to a halt, staring. That hint of concern wrinkling his brow…as if he cared.

Except how could she believe that now?

For an instant, caught in surprise and denial, Ava wanted to believe what she'd learned wasn't true. That Flynn hadn't duped her. That he really loved her.

He stepped through the door and her body reacted inevitably, conditioned to soften with yearning. She gritted her teeth and closed her eyes, hating that her first instinct still was to rush into his arms.

'Ava! Talk to me.'

She opened her eyes as he strode towards her.

'Don't!' Instinctively she stepped back, her arm out to ward him off.

He halted mid-stride, dark eyebrows slashing down. 'What is it? Brayson? Has he bothered you?'

Ava laughed, the sound short and harsh. The man who'd once loomed like a spectre meant less than nothing after what she'd discovered.

'No.' Her voice grated. 'Not Brayson.' She wished he were the sum total of her worries.

'Then what?'

Ava lifted her chin, trying to size up the man who'd turned her life on its head. But he looked the same as ever. Clever, gorgeous, caring.

Caring! Her stomach did a sickening loop the loop.

'How about the fact that you cost me my job?' Her voice rose. 'You *deliberately* got me sacked!'

Flynn blanched.

'Nothing to say, Mr Marshall?' Her voice gave a betraying wobble. Even now she'd hoped that he'd deny it. That there was some other explanation. But that blank stare, that waiting tension, told their own story.

Her stomach plunged, leaving her nauseous with disappointment. *He'd betrayed her.*

'You don't deny it.' Her tone was flat but she kept her chin tilted, refusing to reveal how deeply that cut.

Flynn paced forward a step and Ava backed away, her palm out at arm's length.

Was that hurt in his eyes?

How could she think it? She was done projecting what she wanted to see into Flynn's face and actions. From now on she'd demand the truth.

'That job was draining you.' He spread his arms, as if to show he'd had no ulterior motive. 'I did it for the best.'

'You were looking after me?' She couldn't believe this.

'That's right. I was concerned for you.'

'How *dare* you?' Fury such as she hadn't experienced in seven years gushed in her bloodstream. 'How can you tell me you acted for my own good?' Ava crossed her arms over her heaving chest. 'You who work longer hours than any sane person should.'

Of all the patronising claptrap!

'*I* look after me. *I* decide where I work.' She shook her head. 'You lied to them about me wanting to go.'

'I didn't lie. I merely mentioned we had plans to move out of London and start a family. I offered a donation to the cause.'

'Don't be disingenuous.' Ava threw up her arms. 'You lied to the CEO. Worse, you lied to me.'

Pain crushed her chest. She'd actually been *grateful* to have such a supportive husband during that difficult, disappointing time when she'd lost her job. Tears of anger burned her eyes and she blinked them back.

'I haven't lied to you, Ava.'

Flynn's stiff features told her he wasn't happy. *Tough.*

'You lied by omission. By insinuation. All that time you were comforting me you'd engineered it.' She paced away, unable to stand still. Every inch of her ached. Her fingers dug into her arms like talons, digging for bone. 'How do you think I feel, knowing that behind my back you were pulling strings, laughing at me?'

'I've never laughed at you.'

His voice ground hard and low. It echoed right to her core, resonating in ways that made her weak.

That, even more than the news of his deception, fuelled her ire.

Ava reached the window and spun round.

Once she'd believed she could read Flynn. Now she knew better. He only let her see what he wanted.

She drew a steadying breath. 'You managed my life. You took control of things that were mine to decide. How do you think that feels?' She didn't wait for an answer. 'I spent my first seventeen years having every aspect of my life controlled by a man who didn't give a damn what I wanted or how I felt. I thought I'd escaped that.'

Ava swallowed the searing knot in her throat.

She thought she'd found true love.

Instead she'd been manipulated by a maestro.

Flynn's deviousness surpassed even her father's.

He hadn't demanded. Oh, no, he'd used her love for him to bend her to his will.

She gagged, bending double.

'Ava.'

He stepped close and she stiffened, straightening.

'I'm sorry. It was a mistake.' Dark eyes searched hers. 'I knew as soon as I'd done it. But then it was too late. You don't know how much I've regretted it.'

'Regretted I'd find out, more like.'

His expression told her she'd hit on the truth.

Pain ripped razor-sharp claws through her, tearing

deep. She hunched again, arms tight across her torso to hold in the hurt. For a moment she imagined distress in Flynn's dark eyes. How ludicrous was that? He was an expert at appearing to care, but it was a sham.

'It wasn't just the job, was it?' By sheer willpower Ava kept the words even. 'If it had been only that—some outdated paternalistic idea that you were protecting me—I might even try to understand.'

She paused, watching his gaze sharpen.

A shudder racked her. The contentment and fulfilment she'd found so recently with Flynn were a mirage. Her feelings, her love, were grounded on a cruel lie.

That cut deepest. All this time she'd believed him to be the one man she could trust…

'It was all a hoax, wasn't it?' Hurt chased anger in a furious, boiling brew. 'You never cared for me.'

Flynn stepped in but she refused to back up, merely tilting her chin, her gaze scornful.

'No. You're wrong, Ava. I—'

'Don't *lie* to me, Flynn. I'm sick of it. You've been lying from the first.' She hitched a breath. 'I've done some checking, you see. I know more than you think.'

He stilled, his expression watchful.

'You've been buying those portraits of my family for years. *Years*, Flynn—not just since our wedding.'

That revelation had given her the creeps. It was one thing for her husband to buy a painting of Frayne Hall before they'd met again, since he'd grown up on the estate too. But to buy pictures of *her* ancestors? As if he were already planning for their future together?

'Nothing to say?' She swallowed and forced herself to continue. 'Then there's the Hall itself. It wasn't up for sale, like you pretended. You approached the owner. I dread to think what inflated offer you made to convince him to sell.'

A flicker in Flynn's dark eyes was the only animation in his face. That and the tiny pulsing throb at his throat.

'I can afford it. I knew you'd like living there. It was in your mother's family for centuries, until your father's business collapsed.'

Ava leaned forward, jabbing a finger into his dark red tie. 'But *when* did you offer to buy it? After our wedding? Or...' She paused. 'Or could it be you made an offer before that? Before Prague? Before Paris, even?'

Flynn shrugged. 'Does it matter? It's a wonderful old place—perfect for us.'

The front of the man stole her breath. 'It matters! You let me think you'd bought it because of *me*. You talked about *us* finding a home together, but all the time it was the place *you* wanted.'

'You like it too. Admit it. You've enjoyed being with me at Frayne Hall.'

Ava squeezed her eyes shut. The trouble was he was close to the truth. Living with Flynn at the Hall these past weeks had been as close to bliss as she'd ever come. Not because of their surroundings but because she'd felt they'd finally achieved the happiness she'd sought so long.

A happiness built on deception.

'Don't twist this.' Her eyes snapped open. 'You began negotiations to buy it long before we met in Paris. You began sourcing my family portraits before you met me. You wanted Frayne Hall, but that wasn't enough. You wanted a chatelaine to go with it, didn't you? A Frayne to keep the family connection alive. And I fitted the bill. I was a Frayne by blood, if not by name, and you *targeted* me—just like you targeted all those *things* you wanted to acquire.'

Ava sucked her breath in so hard she couldn't speak. She was crumbling inside, turning brittle and shattering little by little.

Still he said nothing, just watched her.

What had she expected? Some excuse?

There was no excuse for what he'd done.

'I chatted with your PA today. We've become quite friendly lately.'

That got a reaction. Flynn's brows shot up.

'I asked for details of the place you'd stayed in Paris. Said I wanted to surprise you.'

Her smile was tight and painful. It was a surprise all right—just not a romantic weekend away, as his PA had assumed.

'Imagine how I felt when I discovered she'd booked your trip the day after I booked mine.' Her mouth twisted. 'And instead of arranging accommodation for a mere two days, as you'd led me to believe, your PA booked the Paris hotel for a whole week—the exact length of my stay. And—surprise, surprise— she also booked your Prague hotel at the same time. Just as if you already knew my itinerary.'

Ava stared into impenetrable eyes and her fury boiled over. She jabbed at his tie again.

'You planned it all. You planned to stay as long as I did. That meeting on the boat—it wasn't a coincidence. You engineered it.'

His fingers closed around her shaking hand. 'Now, Ava—'

'Don't you "Now, Ava" me! Just admit it.' She tried and failed to free her hand.

'I wanted time to get to know you. The business meetings I had in Paris were real, but, yes…' He drew a slow breath. 'I'd planned to stay on and spend time with you afterwards.'

Ava shook her head. 'But you didn't even *know* me!'

'Of course I knew you. I watched you grow up.'

'That's not the same as knowing me, Flynn.' Even now Ava could scarcely believe what he'd done. 'No sane man plans his vacation to be with a woman he hasn't seen in seven years.' Especially a workaholic like Flynn, who found it hard taking time off. 'Not without an ulterior motive.'

The thought of his ulterior motive churned her empty stomach. She tried again to tug her hand loose.

'You plotted to meet me.' That chilled her. 'You stalked me, planned to stay in the same cities, oh-so-accidentally bumped into me on that cruise.'

'I wanted to get to know you again, Ava. I knew we'd be perfect together.'

His fingers firmed around her hand. They felt ridiculously reassuring.

The realisation scared her.

This time she managed to wrench her hand away.

'There's that word again. *Perfect.*' She spat it out, the taste of it rancid. 'There's nothing perfect about us, Flynn. It was all an illusion.' She choked, her throat convulsing on the word, but forced herself to go on. 'You connived to meet me. What did you do?

Set someone to check my movements? To vet that I was *suitable*?'

A flush tinted his high cheekbones and pain stabbed her.

'It was unconventional, I admit, but—'

'Unconventional?' Her voice rose. 'It was a complete and utter invasion of my privacy. You *lied* to me again and again.'

'I'm sorry.'

The words dropped into the heaving silence. He looked stiff, uncomfortable.

'I didn't mean to hurt you.'

CHAPTER FIFTEEN

DAZED, AVA STARED up at the man she'd thought she knew. 'You didn't mean to hurt me?'

It was too much. She tottered to a chair and sank into it, her bones too brittle to support her.

'How could you think you wouldn't hurt me?' She felt as if she was being ripped apart. 'I can't believe what you've done.'

To her relief, Flynn didn't approach. Finally it must have sunk in that she didn't want his touch. She shivered, realising how addicted she'd become to his caresses. She snapped her teeth shut to stop them chattering.

'I knew I could make you happy.'

Even now it wasn't repentance she heard in his voice, but certainty.

'How? By becoming my father? By using me as he did?'

'No!'

At last the mask cracked. Raw emotion turned Flynn's eyes from impenetrable to burning hot. Deep grooves lined his cheeks. He spun on his foot, marching across to the window and staring out for long seconds. When he turned back his look was bleak.

'I never wanted to become your father. Never that. But I wanted what he'd had.'

'I see.'

Through a cushion of shock she realised he hadn't denied her accusations. That should have shattered her. Some time soon, she knew, she'd fall apart. Ava prayed it wouldn't be in front of him.

'You wanted an aristocratic wife and a big old house and lots of money.'

Flynn shoved his hands into his trouser pockets, his expression bleak. With his feet planted wide and his broad shoulders outlined against the light he looked like some sexy corporate raider. Except it wasn't some far-off company he'd plundered. It was her life.

Ava shivered, huddling in on herself for warmth.

'I wanted the ability to control my life.'

'By stealing mine?'

Pain etched his features. Ava told herself she'd imagined it. *She* was the one hurting.

'It wasn't like that.'

'Then what *was* it like?' Nothing he said would make her forgive him, but she needed to understand how he could have used her so callously.

Flynn's gaze shifted. 'All my life I knew what

it was to be at someone else's mercy. My parents worked hard but money was tight, especially when Dad got sick. They dreamed of moving off the estate into a place of their own. Instead they were wholly dependent on your family for their income and the roof over our heads.'

His mouth tilted in a humourless smile.

'Your father didn't spend money on tenants' cottages, even when he drove a Rolls-Royce. Our quaint little cottage was damp, uninsulated, with antiquated plumbing and wiring that made it a potential death trap.'

His eyes locked with hers and the banked energy in his stare blasted through her cushion of shock.

'It didn't matter how hard they worked, how many hours they put in, they couldn't get ahead. And the hours weren't reasonable.' He shook his head. 'Do you know how many nights my mother worked, preparing for those big house parties?'

Ava could guess. Everything had had to be perfect.

'Night after night she'd drag herself home after midnight. And she'd regularly be up early to cater for breakfast.'

He paused, scowling.

'My father was ill for a long time and his income dried up while the bills mounted. By the time he was hospitalised we were dependent on my mother's wage and anything I could scrounge from odd jobs.'

His mouth tightened to a grim line, and despite herself Ava found herself sympathising. She'd never had to worry about money till she'd struck out on her own, and then she'd been single and healthy. She'd also been extremely fortunate to get a job so quickly at the charity.

'I watched my mother work herself to a shadow—trying to keep everything together, trying to afford better treatment for him. And do you know what thanks she got for her hard work?' Flynn's eyes blazed. 'None. Never a thank-you or a pay rise. And when she needed time off to visit my dad in the hospital your father threatened to sack her if she left in the middle of his fancy winter ball. Even when Dad went into a decline.'

It was the sort of bombastic, unreasonable attitude that had characterised Michael Cavendish. He'd been ruthless, using anyone and everyone to get what he wanted. Of course he'd have threatened the indispensable Mrs Marshall to keep her from leaving during the biggest event on his calendar.

Flynn's fist ground into the palm of his other hand. 'She was afraid if she got sacked she wouldn't be able to support *me*.'

Beyond the raw fury Ava discerned a bewildered,

helpless note she'd never heard from Flynn. It reminded her that he'd been just sixteen when his father had died.

Flynn raked a hand through his cropped hair. 'My father died early on Christmas morning. He'd clung to life the previous day, waiting for her. But in the end he just didn't have the strength to hold out. He died an hour before she got there.'

'You were with him.'

The lift of Flynn's shoulders was jerky, reminding her of the gangly youth he'd once been. 'For what it was worth, yes. But he was waiting for *her*. I was a poor substitute.'

Ava doubted that. She'd seen Flynn with his parents. His presence would have meant a lot to his father.

But *her* father had prevented Flynn's mother being with her dying husband. No wonder Flynn had hated him. Her heart felt so heavy she thought it might split.

'That night I vowed things would change. No more living our lives at the beck and call of your father. No more powerlessness. No more poverty.'

Ava wondered if Flynn even saw her. His expression was haunted.

'With money my father would have got better treatment—the best specialists and care.' He blinked and seemed to focus. 'That night I decided I'd do whatever it took to conquer the world. To have it on my terms so my family and I would always be safe.'

Ava's mouth dried as she saw the glitter in his eyes—hard and unyielding as polished metal. 'You wanted money?'

'More than that. I had to control my environment—like your father did. To have the clout, the respect and authority to manage my world. To keep my mother safe and secure. To keep my family safe and secure.'

His gaze sharpened and focused and Ava read possessiveness in that look. Heat drilled through her.

'I promised myself I'd triumph over your father and men like him. One day I'd take what was his and own Frayne Hall. I'd be richer and stronger, but I'd do it *right*. No trampling on the little people along the way. No sharp practices. Just talent and honest hard work.'

She shot to her feet. 'Honest? The way you've treated me isn't *honest*.' She'd been a pawn in his plan—a cog in the wheel of his quest for power.

He'd never wanted *her*. Just what she represented. Now it all made sense in a terrible, skewed way. Her gorge rose and she had to clear her throat.

'No wonder you're a workaholic. There'll never be enough money to satisfy you, will there? There'll always be the possibility that something will go wrong and you'll lose your fortune—like my father did.'

Ava's laugh was bitter.

'There was I, worrying about the hours you work, worrying it would destroy your health. And all the time it's what's driven you. The need for money.'

Her gaze narrowed. Her stare should have incinerated him on the spot, but he looked as solid and untouched as before.

Something like hatred snaked through her belly.

'But money wasn't enough, was it? You wanted social standing. You wanted prestige. The big house, the aristocratic ties, the socially acceptable wife.'

Ava's breath sawed in tight lungs.

'And my father showed you how to do it.' She spat the words. 'Buy the big house. Marry the daughter with the ancestry and the social connections. Turn her into—' She snapped her mouth shut as nausea rose.

Flynn opened his mouth to speak and she spun away, unable to look at him any more.

'No, you weren't ready to use me like that quite yet, were you?' He'd stood up for her with Brayson, after all. 'What was the plan? To get me pregnant first? Make sure I'd produced an heir or two to your mighty corporate enterprise before you started loaning me out to your business associates?'

'*No!*' The roar stopped her in her tracks. 'I never—'

'Of course you never.' Her shoulders hunched as she stared through the rain at London's blurred outline. The grey misery of the day mirrored her aching soul. 'You didn't know my father had turned my mother into his whore. Not till I told you. But you're adaptable. I'm sure given a couple of years you'd have seen the advantages—'

'Don't *ever*—' hard fingers grabbed her arm and swung her round '—suggest such a thing.'

Flynn loomed over her, his face dark, scored by an anger she'd never seen before. As if her taunt had pierced his non-existent heart.

But Ava was done with being taken in.

'Why not? Because it's beneath you?' She jabbed her finger into his shirt, wishing she could drill deep enough to draw blood the way he'd made her bleed inside. 'You've used me from the first. You've baulked at nothing to get what you want.'

'I told you, it's not like that. I care—'

'*Care?*' She thrust her face into his and read his shock. 'You don't *care*! You never have. I'm just the stupid, gullible woman you manipulated. You've paraded me like a trophy, haven't you?'

She'd just been too blind to see.

'What was I?' Her finger stabbed him again. 'A key to the few doors still shut to you?'

A shadow flickered in his eyes and she knew she'd hit the nail on the head.

Blind fury swamped Ava. After a lifetime of bottling up emotion she'd begun to let go since meeting Flynn. Now her feelings overwhelmed her. She hauled back and aimed a punch at his chiselled jaw. Not some namby-pamby slap, but a punch that would have felled him.

Except he caught her fist in his hand, his fingers closing around hers, stopping her mid-swing.

'Let me go.' She ground out the words between clenched teeth, her chest heaving.

'Not until I'm sure you won't hurt yourself.'

'Hurt myself? It's *you* I want to hurt, Flynn Marshall.' She leaned in, lashing him with her words. 'I never thought it possible to hate someone like I hated my father. But congratulations. You've succeeded. I hate you even more than I did him.'

His face froze. She felt a jolt of something pass through his hands and into her.

'You don't mean that, Ava. It's a shock, I know, and I'm sorry. But I can explain.'

'Explain what? That despite your careful scheming you actually fell in love with me in Paris? That it wasn't a cold-blooded con?' She shook her head.

'Or was it in Prague? Was that when you realised you loved *me*, not just what I could bring you?'

Why she let the words spill out Ava didn't know. They only lashed the open wounds in her heart. Flynn had never loved her. He'd manipulated her at every turn and now he was trying to excuse his actions.

She blinked back the hot prickle of tears, determined not to let him see her cry.

'Go on, Flynn. Tell me you fell in love with me in Prague. After all, it was so romantic. All those roses, and the wedding dress in just my size. How long did you have your poor PA working on that?'

'Ava, don't. You're upsetting yourself.'

She tugged, but couldn't free her hand. 'So I'm upsetting *myself*? Funny, I thought it was *you* who'd done that. What am I supposed to do? Take it all in my stride?'

'You could try listening.'

Ava drew a deep breath and stared into those lying ebony eyes. 'I'm. Never. Listening. To. You. Again.' She huffed a breath. 'Let me go. Now.'

'Not until you've calmed down. You need to hear me out. I care for you, Ava. You must realise that. It started out…differently, but—'

'Differently?' Despite her determination, tears spiked her eyelashes. Tears of pure fury. 'It started out as a cynical scheme to dupe me. To make me fall for you. Don't dare try to tell me you care for me.'

To her horror her mouth wobbled. She despised this weakness she couldn't conquer.

'Let me go, Flynn.'

'Not till you calm down.'

'I'm done listening to you. I'm done with *you*.' He flinched as she leaned into his space once again. 'You've destroyed whatever I once felt for you.' She drew a shuddering breath. 'I'm leaving.'

'You're not going anywhere.' With one sudden move Flynn had her backed up against the full-length window, his big frame hemming her in, his expression fierce.

'You'd use force to keep me here?'

His mouth tugged up at one side in that smile she'd always loved. Her heart pounded faster.

'I don't need force, Ava. You know that.'

He captured both her hands and planted them against his chest, covering them with one of his. His other hand stroked up her side, from her hip to her breast, lingering and making her breath hitch.

'You think you can seduce me?'

He leaned in, his teeth grazing her neck, and she arched back against the reinforced glass, torn between dismay and a terrible need that shocked her to the core. How could she want this man when he'd betrayed her? Yet liquid heat pooled between her legs as his hand strayed to her breast.

'I despise you, Flynn Marshall.'

He squeezed her breast and she bit back a groan.

'No, you don't. You're angry, and I deserve that, but you love me. You know you do.'

He crowded her, his body against her from shoulder to thigh. His erection jutted into the softness of her belly and to her horror Ava wanted to grind her hips against him.

'Not any more. I never want to see you again.'

'Really?' His lips moved against her throat as his hand skimmed her leg, bunching her skirt high.

Some primal part of her revelled in his blatant power even as she berated herself.

How could she want the man who'd used her so?

Yet she did.

The realisation threatened to break her.

'I hate you.'

She closed her eyes, trying to summon the strength to withstand his sensual onslaught. Instead the darkness concentrated every sensation. Her body hummed into overload as his hand slid higher, up her inner thigh, over her lace panties, then delved inside them.

'You call that hatred?'

His voice was a deep burr, scraping her flesh as his fingers probed the dampness between her legs.

'I—' Speech cut off as in one shocking move he curled his hand around her panties and tore them away. Her eyes popped open and she stared into eyes so dark she couldn't tell pupil from iris.

'Tell me you don't want this.' His hot breath grazed her face as his fingers teased her most sensitive spot. Her pelvis circled needily into his touch.

A feral smile curled his mouth. 'You still want me, Ava.'

Anger and despair and a wild, keening need to have him again—just once—drove Ava on. Dragging her hands from his hold, she slipped them down his body, one working the button on his trousers, the other moulding his erection.

Flynn sucked in his breath and that smile disintegrated.

'Yes.' He hissed. *'That.'*

An instant later his trousers were undone and he'd hoisted her high, his hands at her waist. He slammed her up against the window and somehow, without her even thinking about it, her legs were around his waist. His erection was hard against her soft folds. Ava shimmied in his hold, desperate for the press of flesh to flesh.

'You love me...' he gasped.

She shook her head. 'No.' He'd never hear those words from her again. Even if, to her utter despair, she feared they were still true.

He lifted her higher, away from that delicious contact, and she almost moaned her frustration.

Desire consumed her, raw and needy. There was nothing gentle about her feelings. She wanted to ride him till he crashed and burned, wrung out by the blast of passion that had risen out of nowhere.

She wanted to feel one last time that shattering climax. Even though it was with Flynn. *Because* it was with Flynn. For Ava knew it would be the last time.

'You love me,' he whispered, his voice velvet on gravel. 'Say it, Ava.'

She read the agony of restraint on his tortured features. He needed her as much as she did him. She tasted victory at the knowledge, albeit tainted.

She gasped and leaned in, dragging his collar aside and biting him on the neck, then licking the spot. The salt tang of his skin filled her mouth.

He shuddered and suddenly he was there, at her entrance.

'Say it,' he hissed.

With one smooth thrust he pushed high, filling Ava till she felt her heart well. Once she'd believed there was nothing more magical than the way they made love, for it symbolised the feelings they shared.

Now she knew better. This was lust—pure physical hunger. Not love.

It shouldn't feel this good. But it did and she couldn't bear it. She'd never been more potently aroused.

'You love me, Ava.'

Her eyes snapped open. Flynn watched her with a concentration that scoured his face, drawing it tight.

She shook her head.

He thrust again, slowly, and a ripple of delight lit an incandescent trail within her. She grabbed his shoulders and locked her ankles at his back, drawing him to her. She felt a thrill of power as he moved again, jerkily.

Ava bit her lip—anything rather than blurt out the words that had once come so easily.

Flynn's hooded gaze bored into hers. Her chest tightened as her body worked against his. She felt everything—too much. The physical, the emotional. There was heat and power and need, in a jumble she couldn't escape, didn't want to escape. Her fingers dug into him, her grip at his waist tightening as he pounded high and hard.

'You.'

He tilted his hips, rising and sending her into a haze of pleasure.

'Love.'

Another thrust, jerkier this time, that had her tee-
tering on the brink.

'Me.'

One final surge and the cataclysm overtook them
both in a pummelling wave. Her cries of rapture
mingled with his hoarse roar of completion. They
shuddered, clinging together like the last survivors
of a wreck in stormy seas.

And still the waves of ecstasy rippled through her,
through them, convulsing them in pleasure so profound it bordered on pain.

Ava clung. How he stayed upright she had no idea.
Surely all her bones had turned to water.

Stunned, she stared back into fathomless eyes that
pinioned her as surely as Flynn's hands and his big
body.

Ava's head flopped back against the glass. Dimly
she was aware of the fire in her chest as overworked
lungs fought to drag in oxygen.

Since Prague she'd wondered what it would be like
if Flynn let go, gave up the niceties, the gentle tenderness that characterised his lovemaking, and let
her experience that part of him he kept leashed. The
wild, primitive side of his nature.

Now she knew.

She'd thought today's revelations appalling. But the
situation was far worse than she'd imagined.

For what they'd just shared had been the single most thrilling experience of her life.

How was she going to eradicate her feelings for Flynn when she still craved him?

What sort of hopeless, pathetic woman was she?

CHAPTER SIXTEEN

FLYNN SAW THE moment Ava's bright eyes clouded.

He read dismay and, worse, pain there.

She stiffened, and he knew that if she could withdraw physically she would, though they were locked together, their hearts hammering in unison.

A terrible, yawning sense of loss engulfed him as he watched her withdraw mentally instead.

For months he'd basked in Ava's warmth. In the sunshine of her smile. In knowing she loved him. It had been a source of guilt. But far more, a secret pleasure.

He was damned if he'd give that up, no matter how much he deserved her hostility. He'd make her see. He *had* to.

Flynn spun round, staggering to the bed as his undone trousers threatened to trip him. They fell onto the mattress, his weight knocking the air from Ava's lungs. But he made no apology. He knew given half a chance she'd scoot away, watching him with hurt eyes that raked his soul.

Using his bodyweight, he held her captive, stripping her clothes off with one hand, his other snaring hers. Fabric tore. Buttons popped. Her breath hitched; her mouth was a curl of distaste.

But her body and avid eyes told him all he needed to know.

When he tugged at her skirt she lifted her hips so he could drag it free. Her breathing was harsh and fast, not with distress but with excitement. When he brushed her breast as he tugged her bra off she arched up, seeking his caress. He bent and sucked hard at her nipple, rejoicing in her gasp of pleasure.

Yet he had to be sure.

'You want this?' She was naked beneath him as he shucked off the last of his clothes. 'You want me?'

She nodded once.

It wasn't what he wanted. He needed her words in his ears, assuring him she still cared. But that would come. He'd show her how good they were together, convince her to stay and hear him out. Everything would be fine.

Flynn ignored the glissade of ice down his nape at the possibility he couldn't persuade her.

Instead he loved his wife with all the passion he usually tempered. He pleasured her, but his touch wasn't gentle. Desperation seeped into each caress, each kiss, each urgent buck of his body.

His heart smashed his ribs as he fought the need

to lose himself prematurely. He had just enough wits to ensure Ava was with him every step of the way. Her hands shook as they skimmed his damp shoulders, his flanks, then anchored hard on his buttocks.

Yes! She was furious. Disappointed. But she needed him, loved him. It was there in her body's urgent demands, in the sweet hunger of her kiss as they rode the maelstrom together into oblivion.

A lifetime later Flynn stirred.

Never had he experienced the white-hot catharsis that blasted him as he and Ava shattered in each other's arms.

She'd blown him to smithereens and he wasn't sure all the pieces had melded back together.

Despite the gravity of their situation his lips curved in satisfaction. He had some persuading to do, but she must realise they were perfect together. That was what mattered—

A sound penetrated. Reluctantly he opened his eyes.

Ava stood naked at the end of the bed. She was lushly curved, her hair a tangled froth of gold, her skin flushed. She'd never looked more delectable.

'Come back to bed and let me explain.'

Her eyes sliced to his and away. But not before he read the glitter in them. *Hell!* She was on the verge of tears. Flynn hated that he'd made her cry. He hated that he'd hurt her when all he'd wanted was to look after her.

Yeah, after you used her for your own ends.

He jack-knifed up, head spinning. That was when he saw she was shoving her bare feet into shoes.

Flynn scowled. This wasn't the time to enjoy how sexy his wife looked naked in high heels. But that indefatigable part of him twitched with interest.

'What are you doing?' It emerged as a growl.

Ava bent to pick up shimmering silk, then tossed the blouse away when she saw it had no buttons.

Flynn softened his voice. 'Come back to bed, Ava. Let me explain. I did wrong. *Badly* wrong,' he added as her eyes flashed at him. 'But I care about you, sweetheart. I—'

'Don't, Flynn.' Her voice was unrecognisable. Clipped and sharp. 'There's nothing I want to hear from you.'

Bemused, he watched her stalk across the room and scoop something from the floor. The sway of her bare breasts distracted him for a moment. It wasn't till she shrugged on her trench coat that he focused. His nape prickled.

'Ava. Be reasonable. You can't go out dressed like that.'

Blue fire shot from her narrowed eyes. 'Watch me.' Her fingers worked furiously, doing up buttons.

Flynn shifted to the edge of the bed.

'Stop right there.'

'But you can't leave. We need to talk.'

'I'm not interested in anything you have to say. Nothing could excuse what you did.'

For an instant her mouth crumpled and his chest felt as if it was caving in.

'You *used* me. Worse, I let you—because I was busy falling for a mirage. I couldn't see I was following in my mother's footsteps. Even though I'd vowed to be stronger, settle for nothing less than true love.'

She drew in a mighty breath.

'I hate you, Flynn.' The words pierced like poisoned darts, making him flinch. 'And I hate myself for colluding with you. For making excuses for you and being weak and not standing up for myself.'

Panic flared. 'You're not weak. You're strong, Ava. The strongest woman I know.' And she loved him. Surely she still loved him. Wasn't love about forgiveness?

But it wasn't forgiveness he read in her over-bright eyes. It was fury and despair.

It hit Flynn that maybe he'd never convince her. Maybe she'd never forgive him.

Pain racked him, hollowing his gut, churning his belly, weakening his limbs.

'Don't go, Ava. Please. I care about you. More than you know.'

He could stop her. He was stronger. He could force her to hear him out.

Except when she'd finished tying her belt her gaze fixed him like a javelin to the heart. The pain in her face was too much. He couldn't force her.

'You think I'd fall for your empty words? Words are easy. You bend them to your own ends. I repeat: there's nothing you can say to make me stay. Not now. Not ever.'

She spun on one heel and marched out the door.

He should go after her.

He needed her.

He couldn't let her walk the streets naked beneath that coat.

But how to win her back if she wouldn't listen?

Fear crowded and he found himself shaking. A harsh laugh ripped from his throat. The tragic irony didn't escape him. For there was one last secret between them.

He loved her.

All this time when he'd thought he was concentrating on his plans he'd been falling in love with her. Ava had crept into his heart and he'd been too busy to see it.

He braced himself on shaking hands.

He loved his wife.

And if he told her she'd think it was another lie.

How could he win back the only woman he'd ever loved when he'd hurt her so badly she refused to listen?

CHAPTER SEVENTEEN

SPRING HAD COME to Newcastle. Even here in the north the temperature had finally risen. There was more blue in the sky than cloud, and the scent of growing things sneaked into Ava's nostrils.

She felt the sun through her jacket and wondered how many months it would be—or would it be years?—till she felt warm.

She'd picked up the pieces. Moved cities. Found a job. Begun to make friends. Kept busy with evenings at the cinema, with the choir she'd joined, Pilates classes, volunteering at a youth centre. She'd even joined a gardening group, though her garden consisted of two sad little window boxes that didn't get enough sun.

If she kept busy one day her smiles would come more naturally. She'd stop pining for Flynn and the life she'd imagined they'd share.

Flynn.

Her hand twitched on the envelope in her pocket. For months there'd been no contact and she'd told herself it was for the best. He hadn't followed her, trying to persuade her. Of course not. Flynn wanted a wife for show, not a woman craving love.

Ava's pace quickened. The sooner she got to this meeting with his lawyer the sooner it would be over.

She knew what was coming. Divorce.

'Are you sure you don't want tea or coffee, Mrs Marshall?'

'No, thank you. I'd rather not delay.'

The lawyer nodded. 'There's a bit to get through.' She opened a folder. 'We'll start with the papers for Frayne Hall.'

Ava stiffened. 'I have no interest in it. My husband…' Her throat closed. 'My husband knows that. I won't make any claim on it in the divorce proceedings.'

'Divorce?' The other woman looked surprised. 'You're arranging a divorce?'

'Isn't that what this meeting is about?'

'Far from it.' The lawyer shook her head.

'You'd better explain.' Ava didn't like the way her heart had lifted at the other woman's words. As if she *wanted* to stay married to Flynn.

How long before she rid herself of that weakness?

'Mrs Marshall, your husband has signed Frayne Hall over to you.'

'He's done *what*?' Ava's voice was a rasp of disbelief.

'It's here in black and white.' The lawyer spread documents across the desk but Ava was too stunned to focus on them.

'Are you sure?'

'Absolutely, Mrs Marshall.' She pointed to Flynn's signature on the bottom of the pages.

Ava slumped back in her seat. How could this be? She knew what the place meant to Flynn. How he'd worked to get it. The lengths he'd gone to. It had been proof of his triumph over her father and all he represented.

Why give it to her? Guilt?

Hope lit her dark mood but she squashed it. She'd spent too long expecting the best of Flynn.

'I don't want it.'

A frown marred the other woman's brow. 'You'd prefer us to organise its sale? You don't plan to live there? Or pursue the option your husband has investigated?'

'What option? I'm afraid I don't know what you're talking about.'

'My apologies. I'd understood that you were involved...' The lawyer shrugged and slid a fat folder towards her. 'It's entirely your choice what you do with the estate, but your husband has invested a good deal of time and money developing a proposal to use Frayne Hall as a vacation centre for disadvantaged children. All the necessary approvals have been obtained. The project is ready to proceed, if you choose, and of course if you approve the plans.'

Ava stared, stunned, at the papers before her.

She couldn't believe her eyes. Extended kitchen facilities. Improved disabled access. A pool complex behind the stables. An outdoor adventure course on the edge of the woods. A large playground, partly under cover, near the main building. Tennis courts. A go-kart track and skate park. A media centre.

Ava flipped the pages, her amazement growing. It was a bigger, far superior version of what she'd worked on in her old job. There were detailed costings and even a list of preferred suppliers.

'Let me get this straight. My husband...' Ava paused on the word '...is giving me Frayne Hall to use as a children's holiday centre?'

'Not necessarily.' The other woman smiled. 'It's yours to do with entirely as you wish. This—' she waved her hand at the papers that must have taken months of painstaking work '—is just an option for you to consider.'

'And this?' Ava scanned another bundle of documents—a business plan.

'I understand one proposal is to open the Hall's

reception rooms for upmarket functions. That would partly fund the holiday centre, so it's not totally dependent on Marshall Enterprises.'

Not totally dependent on Marshall Enterprises.

The papers Ava held drifted to the table and she sat back, blinking. Her pulse pounded.

'He's personally paying for the upkeep?' This was one shock on top of another. She felt wobbly, her breathing uneven.

'Not quite, Mrs Marshall.'

There. Hadn't she known it? Of course it wasn't true.

'Mr Marshall won't fund it. *You* will, if you agree.'

'Sorry?' What sort of sick joke was this? Flynn must know her income was modest. There was no way she could—

'As well as giving you Frayne Hall, your husband has made arrangements for you to become sole owner of Marshall Enterprises.'

'What?' Ava's voice was a breathless gasp. 'You're not serious. Flynn wouldn't give up his company. It's…'

It was everything to him.

His source of income. His proof of identity. His power base. His stability.

Everything he'd worked for since he was seventeen.

'There's some mistake.'

Ava shoved her chair from the table and strode to the window. The view between the buildings was of the River Tyne, the Baltic Art Centre and the Gateshead Millennium Bridge. But in her mind it was Flynn she saw, his determined jaw, his eyes shrewd.

Flynn lived for business. If he wasn't actually working he was calculating his next commercial move.

'No mistake, Mrs Marshall. Your husband has signed over everything he owns, except the house where his mother resides, to you. You own his company, all its assets and Frayne Hall.'

Ava swung round. 'He wouldn't. I don't know anything about running a business.'

The lawyer was on her feet, pouring coffee at a credenza. 'Sugar? Milk?'

Ava blinked. 'Milk, please.' Dazedly she accepted the proffered cup, bending her head to inhale the rich, familiar scent.

'I can see this is a shock.' The lawyer smiled. 'We'll take our time with the details. But you don't have to worry about anything. Your husband has passed the company to you, but since his resignation as CEO it's been run very competently by expert managers. You're a very wealthy woman, Mrs Marshall. Whether you choose to keep the assets your husband has passed to you or whether you choose to sell. You don't need to decide today.'

Ava clung to the railing on the pedestrian bridge, staring blindly at the river.

The lawyer hadn't exaggerated. She was wealthy beyond her wildest dreams. But it wasn't the money that stunned her. It was that Flynn had cut himself off from everything he cared for. His wealth, his business, Frayne Hall.

Building his empire had been his sole purpose. How could he relinquish it?

Yet it was done. He'd walked away from the lot.

An alarm sounded and the pedestrians hurried away. The bridge was about to lift to let a boat through. Huddling into her jacket Ava followed, her mind in turmoil.

As she reached the end a silhouette caught her eye.

A man looking towards the river. Towards her.

A tall man with wild, windblown curls. A man with broad shoulders and long, powerful legs.

Flynn.

She stumbled to a halt, her heart beating so loudly she scarcely heard the bridge siren.

He didn't move. His hands were deep in his pockets and his feet planted wide, as if to ground himself.

How long had he been watching her?

Ava took a step forward. Then another. There was no conscious decision to go to him but suddenly she was hurrying, drawn by something stronger than caution. Something that made her battered heart lift despite all she'd learned about dreams not coming true.

'It's you.'

He looked different. Like the Flynn she remembered from years ago. In faded jeans and a leather jacket, ebony curls framing a face that was all hard lines. More lines than before. The grooves beside his mouth were deep and his mouth grim. He looked dangerous rather than suave.

Dangerous to her heart. It slammed to a stop as their eyes met, then gave a mighty thump and took off racing.

'Why?' she whispered.

'You told me there was nothing I could say that would make it better.' He shrugged. 'Actions speak louder.'

Ava stared at that taut face. Nothing moved except his hair, riffled by the wind. And something in his eyes. They weren't as impenetrable as she recalled.

She stepped close. His scent drew her and she had to ground her feet rather than lean in.

'You think you can get away with that?'

'Sorry?' His brows rose.

'You don't think I deserve an explanation?' She watched him watch her and something cracked inside. 'You think it's enough to make some ridiculously extravagant gesture and say *nothing*?' She heard her voice wobble and snapped her mouth closed.

One hand lifted towards her, then fell. 'What can I say?'

Indignation swamped her. Lava-hot fury that was unstoppable after what he'd put her through. She'd walked into the lawyer's expecting divorce papers and instead…

'An explanation would be a good starting place.' She struggled for control. 'What made you think I'd want your money, your business? What am I supposed to do with it?'

'Build your dream.' His jaw was clamped so hard his lips barely moved.

'My dream!' She blinked back a hot glaze of tears. 'My dream was never about money. You must know that.'

'You can have your children's holiday home.'

Ava stared. 'You honestly think that was my dream? That it would make up for—' She waved her hand when words failed. Finally she found her voice. 'It's something I believe in, something I want to do, but it's not my life's ambition.'

'Then what is? Tell me and I'll help you get it.'

He looked so earnest she couldn't bear it. She turned to stare blindly at the river, her heart aching. After all this time it was still Flynn she wanted.

'Ava?'

His deep voice came from just behind her. She felt his warmth. She wanted to drink it in. *That* was how successfully she'd banished him from her heart!

'Please. I *am* sorry. That's why I signed everything over to you. I couldn't think of words convincing enough to explain how much I regretted what I'd done. I thought *doing* something like that would show you.'

'Doing something like giving up what you've spent your life working for?'

'Exactly. When I saw how badly I'd hurt you, how I'd turned into someone like your father, I couldn't bear it. I didn't like the man I'd become, with my grandiose plans. It wasn't what I'd intended.' He paused. 'I hated how I'd injured you.'

'So you're sorry?' Ava wrapped her arms around herself, wondering why the apology didn't lighten her leaden heart. Why the stupendous gift didn't assuage the pain. 'I don't want your blood money.'

'You don't?' Flynn's voice sounded hollow.

'It's not enough.'

He was silent so long she thought he wouldn't speak again.

'It's all I had to give.'

Ava hunched forward, pain slicing. Had she really expected anything else? She knew Flynn didn't love her. How could it still hurt? How could she have thought that might have changed?

'Ava!' Firm hands grabbed her upper arms. 'Are you okay?'

He drew her back against him and she wanted to cry out, make him let her go. But she didn't have the strength.

'Please—say something. Are you ill?'

'I'm not ill.' Hot tears tracked her cheeks.

He stepped in front of her, horror dragging his features down as he saw her face. 'Please don't cry. I didn't mean to hurt you again. If you want I'll leave. I just had to see you one more time and tell you I love you. Try to explain—'

'You what?'

Flynn stroked her wet cheeks with his thumbs, his breath warming her chilled face.

'I love you.'

The intensity of his expression rocked her back on her feet.

'I love you with all my heart. I'll do whatever it

takes to make things better for you. Even walk out of your life.'

Wide-eyed, Ava read sincerity in his gaze. Plus fear, pain and determination.

'Is that what you want? For me to walk away and never come back?'

He looked so stricken, a bubble of hope surfaced. He wasn't feigning. 'Why wait so long to contact me?' That still hurt.

'Would you have seen me? You were so furious. Besides, I needed time to arrange all the legal work, to prove you mean more to me than anything.'

'You're just saying what you think I want to hear.'

'You think I'd give up everything I've worked for to someone I didn't care about?' His mouth skewed. 'You're the one with the power now. You own everything I had and it's been done in such a way that I can't lay claim to it if we divorce. I don't even have a job.' His laugh was a short huff of sound. 'I have no hold over you.'

Except for her feelings. Did she dare risk them again after the anguish he'd put her through?

'You feel guilty?' Ava lifted her chin.

'Of course I feel bloody guilty. I injured you—badly.' Flynn's scowl made him look ferocious. 'What's worse is that you're the one person I'd do anything to protect. *I love you, Ava.* More than wealth or success or power.'

'You didn't love me when you married me.' She wanted to believe him but she'd learned caution.

'No.'

Her heart sank.

'That was the plan, at any rate. But by the time I started getting to know you I couldn't just use you for my own ends. Our marriage was about you as well as me. I wanted you to be happy. I wanted to protect you and care for you.'

Like the way he'd made their wedding a romantic dream, and the way he'd held back from making love.

The way he'd tried to manage her life.

'That's not love—that's possession. I'm not a chattel.'

He nodded, gently stroking her cheek, and she had to fight not to give in.

'I learned that.' His mouth kicked up ruefully. 'The way you stood up to Brayson. The way you marched out of the penthouse, naked but for a trench coat and heels!' He shook his head. 'You're a strong, independent woman, Ava. Worthy of respect as well as love. I wanted to tell you that day that I'd fallen in love with you but I knew you wouldn't believe me. Words weren't enough.'

Ava's gaze locked with his and she *felt* the emotion that roughened his voice and made his hand unsteady against her face.

She wanted to throw her arms around his shoulders. Weep and laugh for joy. Elation bubbled, hammering to be released.

'You're not saying anything.' His voice ground low. 'Because you don't love me any more?'

Ava shook her head. 'I still love you, Flynn. I've tried not to, but I can't seem to push you out of my heart.'

'Really?' Something flared in his eyes and suddenly he looked younger, more carefree.

'Really.' Despite her wariness an answering lightness filled her chest, lifting her mood, threatening to sweep her into an ecstasy of happiness.

'But you're not sure.' His expression sobered.

'I've learned…caution. I love you, Flynn. I want to believe you've changed—'

'But it will take more than a grand gesture?'

To her surprise Flynn didn't look daunted or disappointed. His face creased in a grin. She felt its impact right to her core. Just as she felt the heat and gentle pleasure of his fingers weaving through hers.

'Then it's a good thing I'm an expert at persuasion, Mrs Marshall. And that I mean every word.'

He raised her hand and pressed a chaste salute to the back of it. Ripples of delight eddied out from the spot, making her shiver. She still loved him. Was it crazy to hope this time it was all real?

His grin faded, replaced by an expression of determination.

'If it takes years to convince you I've changed, that's fine. I love you with all my heart and I'm looking forward to proving it. Will you let me try?'

A smile trembled on Ava's lips. Self-denial only went so far. How could she turn her back on her chance at happiness?

'If you insist.'

'Oh, I insist, Mrs Marshall. I won't be satisfied till there are no more shadows in your eyes and no doubts in your heart. Till you know I love you absolutely and completely.'

EPILOGUE

'Hurry up, slowcoach,' Ava taunted. 'I promised your mother we'd be in time for an early dinner so we can decorate the tree. She's made herself at home and is cooking up some festive Marshall family treat.'

A Marshall family treat.

Sometimes it still stunned Flynn that Ava was with him, despite the way he'd almost destroyed their marriage.

He paused in the act of dragging the evergreen through the snow. In front of him Ava all but danced up the hill, a vision to warm any husband's heart in ski pants and a jaunty red pullover with silvery snowflakes. The Santa hat she'd worn for the kids down at the Hall still sat sexily on her blonde hair.

She was the only Christmas treat he wanted. The only one he'd ever need. What would he have done if she hadn't given him another chance?

'And Rupert phoned to say he's arrived. He's even painted baubles for the tree. Can you believe it?' She turned and caught him staring. 'What? Am I still wearing that snowball?' She brushed her shoulder, where one of the kids had landed a lucky shot.

Flynn shook his head. Her eyes sparkled brighter than the dazzling snow. Her lips were riper than holly berries. But it wasn't her beauty that poleaxed him. It was her happiness. She was radiant.

And she was his.

'Flynn? What's wrong? Is the tree too heavy?' She plodded back towards him.

He raised his eyebrows. 'What? You think I've turned into a wimp since I gave up my CEO position? Have a little faith, woman.'

If anything he felt more vigorous than ever. Dropping out of the rat race, concentrating instead on the challenges of running the Hall's various enterprises with Ava, was the best thing he'd ever done.

Almost the best thing.

His wife was that. His heart swelled with emotion.

'Flynn?' She was before him now, azure eyes questioning. Her gloved hand covered his. 'There's something wrong, isn't there?'

How she knew, Flynn wasn't sure. Except that they'd become incredibly attuned.

'Is it because tomorrow is Christmas?' Her voice was soft. 'It must be hard…the anniversary of your father's—'

'It's not that.' For the first time in years he hadn't faced the festive season with pain twisting his belly.

'Then what?' Her brow crinkled. 'We've had such a good day with the kids. You were marvellous with them.'

He shrugged. 'I didn't do anything special. It's just that some of them aren't used to having a guy spend time with them. I'm a novelty, like the other male staff.'

Interacting with the kids—some eager for his presence, others initially surly or shy—had made him appreciate the time he'd spent with his father. Only now did he realise how truly lucky he'd been.

It made him hope that one day he and Ava would have children of their own. Not to inherit their mother's sizeable fortune, but to share their lives.

She frowned up at him, her kissable lips a delicious pout. 'Are you going to tell me what's wrong?'

He hefted a breath, filling his lungs with the scent of her. 'Everything's right. So very right I almost can't believe it.'

Flynn took her gloved hands in his, feeling the inevitable leap of connection.

'The question is, is it right for you too? You needed to be convinced about me.'

Flynn's throat closed and he found himself bereft

of words. He'd taken each day as it came, but it was time to know for sure.

'Oh, Flynn.' She leaned in, her eyes wide. 'I'm sorry. I didn't realise I hadn't—' She shook her head. 'I thought you knew how much I care for you.'

'I know you love me.' His voice scraped out. 'I know I love you. I adore you. But am I enough?'

'Absolutely.' The word was a warm benediction on his face. 'I trust you, Flynn. Completely. You've proved time and again that you're a bigger man than the one I married. That it's people who matter to you—like me and your mother and those kids down there. You're not hung up on money or status.'

Her eyes glowed.

'I admire the man you are now: honest, compassionate and fair.' Her mouth twitched. 'And you don't keep secrets any more.'

Flynn nodded, the tightness in his chest easing. His last secret—the fact that he'd ensured Benedict Brayson had no future in the City of London, nor in the UK—he'd shared with Ava months ago.

Her gaze searched his. 'The question is, am I enough for you?'

Flynn wrapped his arms around her, hauling her close. 'You're all the world to me.' There was nothing he wanted more than to be with Ava for the rest of his life. 'I never knew life could be this good.'

'Me neither. I'd always hoped…' she shook her head '…but until now I wasn't sure. You make my world better. I love knowing you're there for me.'

'Always.' He cradled her face.

'Promise?'

'I promise.' He smiled into her eyes, his heart full. He leaned down and pressed his lips to hers.

Long minutes later, when they pulled back, Flynn's chest was heaving, his pulse racing. He held her to him, never wanting to let her go.

Ava glanced up the hill at the glass and oak-framed house they'd designed together. It sat in her favourite glade, part of the estate but separate from the Hall.

'It's a pity our guests are waiting.' She snuggled in to him, her nose cold against his neck.

Flynn trailed his hand up her sweater. 'They'll wait a little longer. This calls for an early celebration.'

'I wish we could.' She laughed.

His hands moved.

'Flynn!' She gasped, her eyes rounding. 'Not here.'

'Where better,' he murmured against her throat, 'for a little wildness?'

Fat flakes of snow drifted down as he backed her against a sheltering tree, holding her tight.

'You can't!' But her body arched into his, her voice breathless with laughter and excitement.

'So you want me to stop, Mrs Marshall?' He made as if to pull away.

Instantly firm hands stopped him. 'Later, Mr Marshall. Much later.'

Flynn chuckled, heady with joy.

He was the luckiest man in the world.

* * * * *